STO

LOVE'S SECOND BLOOMING

After the tragic death of her husband in a car crash, Serena is left with only the joys of her young son, Nicky, and her fascinating job with old Walter, an esteemed wine importer. Then suddenly into her life comes the dark and brooding Roberto and his acid-tongued sister, Lucia. Both want to take her adored son back to Italy, but Serena trusts neither of them. What can her future possibly hold now?

GRACE GOODWIN

LOVE'S SECOND BLOOMING

Complete and Unabridged

LINFORD
Leicester

First published in Great Britain in 1994 by
Robert Hale Limited
London

First Linford Edition
published 1996
by arrangement with
Robert Hale Limited
London

British Library CIP Data

Goodwin, Grace
    Love's second blooming.—Large print ed.—
Linford romance library
1. English fiction—20th century
I. Title II. Series
823.9'14 [F]

ISBN 0-7089-7888-6

Published by
F. A. Thorpe (Publishing) Ltd.
Anstey, Leicestershire

Set by Words & Graphics Ltd.
Anstey, Leicestershire
Printed and bound in Great Britain by
T. J. Press (Padstow) Ltd., Padstow, Cornwall

This book is printed on acid-free paper

1

SHE rose from her desk and went to look out over the river, her brows creased with worry. It seemed that her younger sister, Danielle, had been a worry to her ever since she could remember.

In repose, Serena's face was fair-skinned, smooth and calm, her blue/green eyes expressive as was her lovely mouth. With fine cheekbones and a long slender neck, her beauty matched her name and would be little changed by the passing years. But just then there was a troubled, pensive look in her eyes as she stood there, biting her bottom lip and gazing sightlessly out of the long windows that overlooked the Thames. It was a familiar view, one that had never ceased to charm. It had been her consolation ever since she had come to work some ten years ago for Walter

Tunnicliffe, the last of a long line of wine merchants and importers.

Situated on the bank of the river, roughly between two of London's famous old bridges, the vast, high-arched warehouse had not changed much in the last hundred years. Except for the busy little fork-lift trucks below unloading a huge juggernaut of pallets of cases of wine bottles instead of a boat carrying large casks as they had years ago, little had changed. The high roof, the slate-slabbed flooring, the racks and racks of shelving — yes, it seemed exactly as it had been the day the nervous young Serena Weston had begun her first job at sixteen.

Diligently, faithfully, she had worked hard to progress from tea girl and general dogsbody to the present, when she was old Walter's 'right hand man' according to him. At the thought, her face softened. The fondness she had for her boss was returned tenfold. Unmarried and childless, Walter Tunnicliffe loved this cool-looking, slim girl as he would

2

a precious daughter. Although they shared every other confidence, Walter had never ever told her why he hadn't married and Serena, suspecting a deep sorrow, had never asked. Sufficient that she could turn to Walter for anything, whether it applied to business or her private life. And God knows, there was plenty in that to trouble her she thought ruefully.

With a faint sigh, she turned from the window and put the kettle on to make coffee. As she did, Walter came in, the thick old door creaking as always.

"Serena, there's someone to see you." And from the smile on his florid, round face, she guessed who it was. Walter made no secret of his approval of the thickset young man who followed him through the door.

"Matthew — you're back!" Her face alight with pleasure, she reached across to kiss his cheek. "Give me your coat. I'm just about to make some coffee."

As she bustled about, Walter beamed at them both.

"I'll leave you two to catch up then. I want to see you soon though, Serena, about that Chianti order." Still looking at Matthew, she nodded.

"OK Walter."

It was three weeks since Matthew had left for Edinburgh on business and she had missed him. Once they were alone, he reached out, and taking her by the shoulder, turned her for his kiss.

"It's been ages, Serena . . . " His voice thickened, his brown eyes darkening with longing. He had wanted her so long now and yet he realized that they were no nearer to being together as ever they had been. Passing him a mug of coffee and taking one for herself, she sat down on the old leather settee and patted the seat beside her.

"How did it go?"

Matthew, a solicitor, had been on business for an important client.

"Not bad. But it was cold up there;

4

I'm glad to be back, Serena. How's things with you? And how's young Nicky?"

She paused before answering, her eyes clouding again with worry.

"I'm fine and so's Nicky — growing taller and brighter everyday."

"Good," he replied, and yet deep down, she knew that having a seven-year-old son didn't really please Matthew. Turned forty, perhaps he felt too old for children? At least, his awful mother never ceased to tell him so. "But I can see something's worrying you, isn't it? Want to tell me about it?"

As she shook her head, the lovely blonde hair swung bell-like around her slim shoulders.

"Come round tonight for a while, Matthew. I won't keep you, you must be tired."

"M'm, I am, a bit. All right, I'll see you about eight. That do?"

"Please, and oh, Matthew, it is nice to have you home." Once more she reached up and kissed his cheek.

Thickset and a wee bit staid, Matthew looked just what he was — a rather settled, solid solicitor, but his plumpish face was somewhat redeemed by the warm, soft brown of his nice eyes. Serena was fond of him, but would she want to marry him — if she was free? She couldn't help knowing that that was what he was hoping for, but . . .

Walking with him to the door, she said softly, "See you later then. 'Bye for now."

Taking her notepad, she ran lightly down the well-worn stairs to the street level. At the far end, overlooking a busy road, the windows were small and barred; the one thick door had a grille for safety. There she found Walter, the fluorescent lights revealing the pink of his scalp through his white hair as he sat at his oak desk, papers piled high around him.

Three sides of this office, retailing and wine-tasting room had long oak counters, smoothed by a century of wear. Above these were labelled racks of odd bottles of every type of wine, cut-glass wine and liqueur glasses, small tasting cups, all the accoutrements of the busy wine merchant.

"You wanted to see me about something, Walter?"

He straightened his back and ruffled through the papers.

"This invoice is wrong, pet. It says it's for Chianti classico . . . "

"So — that's what I ordered from them," she answered, recognizing the invoice heading.

"Aye, but I've just broached a case. There's no black cockerel round the neck of those flagons," he pointed out wryly.

"It's not a classico . . . ?"

"No. Made in exactly the same way, but it's from outside the classico area. Don't worry, my dear," he added quickly, "we'll keep it; we can move it easily enough. Just drop them a line to put the matter right, m'm?"

"It's not often they make a mistake,"

Serena mused, a crease in her smooth forehead. Had *she* made the error? Lord knows she'd had a lot on her mind lately. If Walter was thinking the same thoughts, his warm smile and soft voice covered them.

Back at her own desk, she found it hard to settle down to her work and was almost thankful for the phone's interruption. That is until the caller finished with "Thank you. 'Bye, Mrs Ercoli . . . "

Mrs Ercoli! Sometimes she hated the very sound of that name. Wished she'd never heard of it. And she had to face it; how she wished it didn't still belong to her. She leaned her chin in her cupped hands remembering . . . it had all started at this very desk . . .

"May I see Signor Tunnicliffe, please, *signorina*?" It was a warm sunny day; a day for dreaming alongside the river with someone — someone just like the good-looking young man watching her with dark eyes full of admiration. In three weeks' time the young Serena celebrated her coming of age, her eighteenth birthday.

"Signor . . . ? Oh yes, Mr Tunnicliffe." She pulled herself together, looking up at the caller with dream-filled eyes. Anyone could see he was a foreigner — Spanish, Italian or something Latin. His hair was really black, and his eyes were the darkest she'd ever seen, with lashes inches long. What a waste on a chap, she mused.

"*Si*. May I see him, please?" He passed her a thickly embossed card.

"The House of Ercoli," she read. "Oh yes, I know — we buy from you." He smiled at her with a flash of even white teeth.

"*Si, signorina*, I know," he replied softly. And feeling stupid, the blush stained her cheeks.

"I'll — er — find out if he can see you, shall I?" And she scrambled out of her seat; for once she'd lost her serenity, shaken by the look in those dark eyes.

Two minutes later, she was back to

tell him, "I'm sorry, Mr Ercoli, he's got someone with him. He'll be about ten minutes . . . " Had she known it, as she looked up at him her blue eyes were begging him to stay — to spend those ten minutes with her.

"*Scuzate*, then I will wait perhaps? *Io sono Italiano*. I am Italian. *Parla Italiano*?" Two dark eyebrows rose in query as he watched her face closely.

"Yes — er, no . . . " She swallowed hard and then began again. "Yes, please wait, Mr Ercoli. No, I'm afraid I don't understand much Italian." Then she smiled radiantly. "But your English is very good." He pulled up a seat, sat with slim legs crossed negligently and began to chat with her, bewitching her with his charm, his good looks and easy manner. Making her feel beautiful and attractive.

All too quickly her boss's caller was gone and the Italian had to leave her. Leave her bemused, her young heart thudding with an excitement she'd never known before. She sat waiting,

10

her eyes like stars, until he came out of the office.

"*Scuzate*! I am to come back again tomorrow, *signorina*. Maybe we talk some more then?"

"Er — yes . . . "

"*Grazie, addio.*"

"'Bye now."

It seemed ages until the same time the next day. They greeted each other like old friends, she laughing at his Italian phrases, he explaining them gently, like the time he pointed up to the small barred window.

"*Soldino do cielo* . . . only a pennyworth of sky for you, *signorina* — "

As he paused, his dark brows raised in query, she told him breathlessly, "Serena. I'm Serena Weston."

He repeated the name carefully. "Serena . . . little Serenita." And her name had never sounded so beautiful. "Me, I am called Gino — Gino Ercoli, the second son of the House of Ercoli."

There was pride in those last words

11

and she realized how wide was the difference between his world and hers.

So had begun the swift, passionate love affair between this son of a large Italian wine-making family and the young Serena.

"You will come to my birthday party, won't you, Gino? My parents would like to meet you and so would my sister, Danielle. I've told them so much about you."

It was hard to be so insistent, to pin Gino down to agreeing. So hard, when he was kissing her, caressing her until she didn't know what she was doing. For, in the three weeks after their first meeting, they had been out together every night. Met for lunch; spent every spare moment together. Yet to Serena there were still too many hours between; empty hours, when she longed to be with him, in his arms, thrilling to the soft words he whispered in her ear in that exciting accent of his.

To Gino, so experienced in the art

of chasing girls, the cool, blonde looks of this lovely English miss was a special challenge. He knew it would take all his persuasive charm to get her into his bed!

For her birthday, he sent her flowers, masses of them, and their fragrance in the office blotted out for once the ever-pervading aroma of wine.

"He's certainly rushing you, Serena love." Walter watched the soft blush, the shining eyes of the young girl who was so dear to him. He was afraid for her. To him, she had never seemed as streetwise as so many girls of her age. There was such an aura of innocence, an untouched air about her, and he truly wanted her to keep that naivety for a little longer.

Gino picked her up early from the little flat she had rented above the warehouse. While she finished dressing, he touched first one birthday card and then another, looking at the little gifts she'd been given that day by her colleagues.

"Will I do?"

As he turned, he caught his breath. She looked truly beautiful! Her dress in midnight-blue made her hair almost silver; the skin of her neck and face seemed like fine porcelain. For her, it was a more sophisticated frock than usual, with the low neckline showing the tender cleavage of her firm young breasts.

"Serena *mia*, you look so beautiful." His voice was thick with desire. "I want you so — *io ho fame*. I am hungry for you, *piccina*." The words came incoherently hoarse with the passion that racked him then.

Just for a second she was scared. They were alone up there and she was suddenly nervous. Afraid, too, of the longing inside her to give Gino what he wanted. After all, she was eighteen today — truly a woman! And it was a woman's longing that made her whole body ache with a depth of yearning that frightened her.

"Don't spoil my make-up, Gino

darling. It took me ages." Her light laugh didn't quite make it, but he released her reluctantly.

Feeling in his pocket, he brought out a thin, velvet-lined box.

"With my love, for you — for your birthday."

"Oh, Gino, it's gorgeous!" The delicate little bracelet was in filigree gold with tiny deep-blue stones.

"To match your eyes, *mia bellissimo, il braccialetto*." As he clasped the bracelet round her wrist, she felt his fingers tremble and the air between them seemed to be filled with the intensity of their feelings.

Of course her father and mother had liked him. No one could resist Gino Ercoli when he set out to charm. Her sister Danielle at sixteen had flirted with him outrageously, lapping up his flattery like a young kitten with a saucer of cream.

"He's a rather gorgeous young man, Serena, my pet, but for goodness sake watch yourself. Don't go overboard for

15

those come-to-bed eyes of his, will you?" In the kitchen later, her mother had tried to keep her words light, but there was a trace of anxiety in the blue eyes so like her daughter's.

But was it too late? Serena wondered if she could ever resist Gino's kisses, his caresses? That night, it was so hard to refuse him. The touch of his lips, his hands, set her whole body alight.

"Let me love you, *cara*. I want you so . . . " His husky pleas almost made her surrender.

"I — I can't, Gino. Oh darling, I do so want to, but I can't — not yet . . . "

"Then marry me!" Before he could stop himself, could control his desire for this silver-haired, fair-skinned girl, the words were out. "Be my *bella moglie*, my dearest one," he begged.

For just a moment she paused, and then with shining eyes and beating heart, she accepted.

"Your wife? Oh yes, Gino! I want that too."

"So, little one, I can stay here tonight?"

She swallowed hard, shaking her head, her eyes begging for his understanding.

"Please Gino, let's wait now. That's what I've always wanted to do — to know that my husband was the first one with me. Please, dearest, say you understand," she pleaded softly.

And Gino, used to the custom of the virgin bride in his own country, understood and reluctantly agreed.

"But we must marry soon — next week maybe?"

"Next week! Oh Gino, we can't."

"*Perchè*? Why?"

"Your folks — they've not even met me yet. And my mother — she'll want a big wedding . . . "

He gave a typical Latin shrug of the shoulders, dismissing her qualms as just so many silly obstacles.

"I — we can't wait for the big wedding, *cara mia*. As for my family, they will never like me to marry any but an Italian girl, so we tell them when it is all done, *si*?" His hands gestured airily, casting aside all her doubts.

And so they were married at the nearby Registry Office with just two strangers as their witnesses. Serena wore the blue dress, a matching hat with a little veil covering her smooth forehead, her lovely hair for once in a thick coil on her slender neck. A posy of white rosebuds clutched in nerveless fingers, she looked so young, so innocent.

They spent their one-week honeymoon in the Cotswolds and if her new husband's lovemaking left her slightly bewildered and unsatisfied, Serena told herself she would learn — they both would, together.

Their first breakfast together was brought up by the pert young waitress from the dining-room below. They had been given the bridal suite at Gino's request, and they sat up, trays across their knees, under the high silken canopy of the four-poster bed. The smell of flowers was everywhere; the sun filtering through the long glass windows had revealed Serena's pink cheeks as the waitress wished them, "Good morning, Mr and Mrs Ercoli." Mrs Ercoli! She was a wife, a grown woman.

Her next thought had made her ask, "Where shall we live, Gino?"

"Ah, ready to be the little housewife, *si*?" he teased. "And this our first day married!"

"Well, we haven't discussed anything sensible yet."

"Sensible! Pah, who likes this sensible?" He made a grab for her, almost upsetting his breakfast tray.

"No, I mean it, darling."

"Well, you stay in your apartment the same. Me — well, I shall be travelling as usual all over Europe to sell my family's wines. In between — every possible moment, I shall come to you, my beautiful new wife."

"I'll have to ask Mr Tunnicliffe; it's his place, you know. We'll need a new bed. Mine's so small." At that, Gino burst out laughing.

19

"Good, I see you have the right order of things. A new bed — yes, that is the most important!"

"Stop it. Oh, let's get rid of these trays." Impatiently she pressed the bell, and that time when the waitress came, she hadn't blushed.

★ ★ ★

"Of course, my dear. Lord knows there's enough room for an army up there. If you and Gino mean to stay on here, we'll have to see about some conversions, m'mm?"

"Walter, you're a pet!" Serena couldn't help but give him a hug. "That's settled then. Now what about those clarets? Have you decided yet?"

Determined not to let her marriage interfere with her job, Serena started as she meant to go on.

That her marriage wasn't working out at all as she had dreamed it would, she kept to herself. How could she explain to anyone — her mother, Walter — that her new husband's lovemaking still left her dissatisfied, disappointed, still wanting . . . something more? How could she tell anyone how often, as Gino turned over and went to sleep, she still lay with her whole body aching for something she wasn't quite sure about? Gino took his own gratification, not caring one jot that she had not reached the height, the peak she should have.

She hadn't really thought too of how lonely she would be when he was away. She didn't feel quite right now with her young friends. They were free to do as they liked; to meet other men; to come and go as they pleased, dancing the nights away.

She found herself waiting, listening every evening for Gino's telephone call. At first, he got home every few days, and their rooms above the warehouse were their own private paradise. Serena was a terrible cook and it was mostly Gino who made them the Italian dishes she soon began to enjoy. Or they would dine out but after living in first one hotel and then another, he preferred to eat in and then go out to a show, or to dance to a good group. Money seemed to be no object to him and she soon learned that her new husband came from a very rich background indeed. As well as acting as a representative, he was more or less responsible for the small but de-luxe office in central London. Sometimes he rang from there to tell her he was coming home.

At others, she would hear the busy chatter of some foreign exchange before his voice finally came through as clearly as if he was in the room with her.

"*Scusi*, little one, there is much fog here. I cannot fly to you yet."

Swallowing her disappointment, she would send him her love.

"*Che duri per sempre, cara.*"

"What does that mean, Gino?"

"May it last forever, dearest. I must go. *Ciao, mia bella moglie*. And you know what that means?"

True to his word, her boss had arranged for much of the top floor to be converted into a really comfortable apartment for the young couple, whilst charging Gino only a fairly modest rent. Firstly came the soundproofing. Several bedrooms and a bathroom were created at the end overlooking the road, with a kitchen and breakfast-room towards the middle. At the other end, a lounge and dining-room was converted to overlook the river. No expense was spared.

And having seen what had been achieved by the architects on the dockside conversions, Walter gleefully described to them the idea he'd had for a lovely big balcony/conservatory overlooking the river. It would be entirely enclosed against inclement weather, with sliding shutters against too much sunlight.

Serena had plenty of time during her lonely evenings to plan just how she would furnish it all. And Gino saw to it that she had enough funds to do so. It seemed to take ages; even doing one room at a time made an awful mess!

But gradually only the balcony had to be finished. Gino hardly ever seemed to be home and she worried. Had he tired of her already?

Did he suspect that their lovemaking wasn't quite as satisfactory for her? That he felt that for her there should be something more? Where was that heaven-shaking experience that her friends had giggled about? If only she knew more; had someone to talk to? She knew she had led a rather sheltered life, going straight from a girls' school to work for Walter.

Whenever his office informed her that Gino would be home, she would spend ages trying to decide what to wear, what to cook; just how to ask all the questions that had been plaguing her since they had last been together.

"Oh, Gino, I've missed you so." She threw herself into his arms, needing his love, his support.

"And I also, *cara mia*. Let me look at you. I swear you get more lovely every day."

Later, limbs entwined, languorously lazy after their lovemaking, she tried to ask him.

"Have you told your people about us yet, Gino? What did they say?"

She felt him grow tense beside her and then his shrug. Quietly she waited, hoping this time to pin him down to an answer.

"I saw them last week . . . " From the tone of his voice, she guessed he didn't want to talk about it.

"You were in Italy. I didn't know." And suddenly Serena realized how little she really knew of her husband's movements.

"A flying visit only, little one. But no," he added angrily, "they do not want to meet my English bride. And so we shall wait — until they get used to the idea; they will — soon, you'll see."

If only she could believe him. Look at how her own parents had reacted . . .

She telephoned her parents every week, and when she rang to tell them excitedly about her marriage, she had hardly begun when she heard the strangled gasp from the other end, then the clatter as the phone fell.

"Mum — are you there? Oh please, Mum, don't be angry. We wanted a quiet wedding — without any fuss or long waiting."

"Serena, how could you?. You're so young. Did — did you have to get married?" How old-fashioned her mother had sounded.

"Of course not! No, we love each other and wanted to be together."

"I just *can't* believe it, Serena." Her mother's voice sounded choked with tears. And for a brief moment she regretted her hasty marriage. "How could you do such a hole-in-the-corner thing? Without telling us — without us being there? Oh Serena, right now I feel I'll never forgive you."

"No — oh, please Mother, don't say that."

"Goodbye for now. I can't think straight." And with that, the line had gone dead, leaving Serena standing, the receiver clutched in her cold hands, tears streaming down her face. And now Gino's folks were rejecting her too . . .

She got out of bed, feeling numb with misery.

"I must get ready for work, Gino."

"You are working today — my first day home for so long?"

"Just this morning, darling. I'll see you for lunch anyway."

When she was ready to go, she found he had turned over and was curled up, fast asleep. She dropped a soft kiss on his cheek, fondly admiring the long, thick, black eyelashes lying on it. Perhaps he was tired, had been working hard?

It was later when she was querying a delivery of Tuscany wines that she saw it — an Italian newspaper left beside the coffee machine by the driver of the huge juggernaut. She had recently started Italian language classes, so she picked it up eagerly, ruefully thinking how far she had to go before she could read a newspaper like that one! As she turned the pages to scan the pictures, she was amazed and delighted to see Gino's face!

It was amongst a gathering of vignerons — wine-growers at a formal reception. But who was the dark-haired beauty on his arm, gazing up into his laughing face with such adoring dark eyes? She was young, perhaps as young as Serena herself, and she looked rich and pampered and happy. They seemed almost to be a pair of lovers! And for the first time in her life, she felt the cruel deep thrust of jealousy's knife.

She rushed up to the apartment to find Gino eating a slice of toast, still wearing his heavy silk dressing-gown.

"Who's this, Gino?" She thrust the paper at him. "This girl with you here?" Her breast rose and fell with the force of her angry breathing. At the sight of the annoyed frown on his face, she realized at once that she'd made a mistake; that this wasn't the way to handle Gino at all!

"Let me see. Oh that one — just the sister of one of the growers there. Why are you . . . ?"

Then he saw her trembling bottom lip, the moist tears glistening in her eyes, and he gathered her close to him, cuddling her face into the silken folds of his dressing-gown, so that she wouldn't see his eyes.

"*Carissima mia*, she was no one, just someone I danced with once only, wishing it was you in my arms. Foolish little one, you know I love only you." And so he smoothed away her fears, with kisses and soft words. But as time went by, those fears grew.

Especially when she found she was pregnant. What would Gino say? They had been married such a short time. She hugged her secret to her heart. Perhaps now her mother would come round to forgiving her, to understand, when she heard about the baby?

Gino was over the moon. In true Italian style, he strutted like a peacock, his masculinity proven, a son on the way!

"We'll have a son, many sons, and then a girl for you," and Serena thought her heart would burst with happiness. How foolish she'd been to worry so. She had too much time alone, she told herself.

When her employer found her one day leaning over her desk, distressed by the awful nausea of morning sickness, he guessed at once what was causing it. His eyes were full of concern; she was so young, a mere child herself.

"You'll have to take great care of yourself now, my dear." And in his usual quiet, caring way, he found her Lettie Davis.

"This is Mrs Davis, Serena. She is looking for a live-in post. I thought she'd do for you. I don't want you to be up there — " he raised his bushy eyebrows — "on your own — not now. The largest bedroom will do as a bed-sitter for Mrs Davis, and she'll stay with you until after your baby comes."

Serena looked at the pleasant face of the tall, middle-aged woman standing quietly at Walter's side.

"I — I don't know," she said with misgiving, "I ought to ask Gino first."

"I did, the last time he was home, and he agreed."

"Oh . . . good. But I could have managed you know."

"I'm sure you could, my dear, but I want you to stay on working as long as possible, Serena. Will you?"

Her eyes wide with gratitude, she told him, "Of course! Walter, you're such a pet." He smiled contentedly, and so had Lettie Davis, the lonely widow. And in a few days, it seemed as if Serena had known her always.

As she grew rounder and more clumsily pregnant, it seemed that Gino was hardly ever at home, and she knew he was seeing other girls. He hardly ever bothered those days to conceal his philandering. Why should he? He had been brought up to understand that a woman should be content to stay at home, have a baby regularly, especially sons, while the man of the house had his 'pillow friends' where and when he chose. As the child grew inside her, so the love for its father died.

When her little son was born a few days after her twentieth birthday, Serena transferred all her love to him. He was so like Gino, she felt an ironical laugh clutch her throat; the same black hair, the large dark eyes and long lashes. Gino was so proud of him; he expected to be the father of lusty sons, but for once, Serena was adamant. From then on she slept alone. After all, Gino made no pretence; he had tired of her now anyway. She was no longer his cool little virgin, but a mother and his fickle heart had found other playmates.

"There's no way I'm risking catching some horrible disease from you, Gino!" she had cried from behind the locked door of the bedroom.

His voice had been thick with anger as he kicked the door.

"But I shall not divorce you, Serena. No — there's no divorce for me, you know that!" And later, before he left once more, they had laid down the terms, the ground rules, coldly like two strangers.

She would go on as usual, working for Walter, bringing up her son with Lettie's loving help. *He* could do as he pleased, see Nicky whenever he wanted. She would bring the boy up knowing he was half-Italian, and he would have all her love.

At twenty, Serena had finally grown up, almost despising the foolish child she'd been only two years before. And to her relief, Gino, who couldn't face her rejection, never bothered her again for his marital rights. He kept her supplied with funds in her bank account; used the apartment as an overnight stop occasionally, and adored his son. He made no secret of his many lady loves. There was never any mention of Lettie's leaving.

It was a barren life really for one so

young, but as little Nicky grew into first a sturdy toddler and then to a bright, handsome little boy, she had been contented. Her knowledge of the wine trade had grown too, along with the Italian language, and now she really was Walter's 'right hand man'. Actually as he grew older, he had left more and more of the running of Tunnicliffe's in her capable hands.

And Serena loved it; loved the ever-present aroma of wine and sunnier climes, of the huge lorries, the sound of bottles clinking, the sight of the Thames and the boats on the river below. Lettie was her friend and mentor; never usurping her place as Nicky's mother, yet caring and loving him dearly . . . With a jerk, the sound of one of the clerk's voices at her elbow brought her back to the present.

"Er — sorry, Tom. I was miles away."

The young man laughed indulgently. "I could see you were, Mrs Ercoli. It's just about this hotel order. Do they

34

want it all delivered, or are we to keep some stock here for them?"

And Serena found herself back at work, the sad memories put aside. It was only later as she prepared to go upstairs for lunch that she remembered Matthew's visit — she must tell Lettie . . .

Dear Matthew — he would want an answer, and she wasn't ready to give him one, was she?

It had been about twelve months ago, she recalled with a smile. The sun had dappled the water just as it did today, and even the street end of the premises had been lighter than usual as Serena worked there. Suddenly the old-fashioned bell had clanged and she looked up to see him standing there, gazing round him, interested and alert.

"Can I help you, sir?"

"Um? Oh yes, I'd like to talk to someone about drinks — wine, spirits and so on." His voice was friendly and Serena liked the look of him. He'd seemed rather put out at finding a girl dealing with his order. He was quite a bit older than herself, she mused. With nice brown eyes and a pleasant smile. A little staid and rather thickset, but yes, she liked the look of this Matthew Jamieson.

"I find myself elected as controller of my club's bar," he began diffidently, "checking orders, accounts, and so on, as part of the house committee. It's all so new to me, but one of the members told me to see Walter Tunnicliffe."

He raised thick eyebrows, looking round as if for Walter, and Serena's face lit up with a smile.

"I can assure you, sir, I'm quite able to help you."

"Yes. Yes, quite," he floundered. "I didn't mean . . . " Such a simple beginning, but it flowered into a deep and warm friendship on Serena's part, and a loving anticipation on Matthew's part.

Divorced, and living once more at his mother's home, he had been a pleasant and gentle companion to begin with, taking her out to dine, to shows. On some Sundays, they had taken young Nicky on picnics and outings. And she had been amused to see how awkward and constrained Matthew was with her son. Young children were strange animals to the sober solicitor. He preferred to forget that Gino was still in her life, and secretly wished that he could ignore the child too. After all, he never discussed his ex-wife with her, did he?

His goodnight kisses had become more and more passionate and Serena knew he wanted her in his bed; knew it was time for their relationship to move on, to deepen. But was *she* ready for that? She was fond of him, would hate to be without him in her life. But for her there had been no blinding passion as there had been when she'd first met Gino.

Perhaps that was a good thing, she mused. At forty-plus, Matthew was so different. Besides, she didn't want someone like Gino again, did she? She only knew that she was beginning to need a man, to love and caress her, to sleep with and bring her somnolent body to life again. She would be twenty-six soon; wanted another child passionately. But was Matthew the one? He didn't seem to understand children, but that would probably come with a child of his own.

She sighed and locked her desk, worrying about the decision she would very likely be asked to make that night. She went to check that the night watchman had arrived and then took the lift up to her home above.

2

SHE found young Nicky busily trying to fit together a complicated jigsaw puzzle on the lounge carpet. He looked up, his dark eyes bright with mischief.

"Ciao, Momma, come sta?" It was a little game they often played — throwing scraps of Italian at each other. At seven, Nicky was much more fluent than his mother for it had been his second language all his young life.

Serena's answering smile was tender as she reached down to ruffle his dark curls.

"Ciao, Nico, piccolo mio." But much as she longed to, she didn't make the mistake of kissing him — he thought that far too sloppy! "How was school today?"

"Ugh!" She almost laughed aloud at his expressive shrug, so Latin, so like

39

his father's! In fact, in Nicky, Gino had his replica in miniature. He wasn't a tall child for his age. Rather, his limbs were compact and lithe, but as he was growing older, he was becoming more and more like Gino and there were times when Serena wished he wouldn't! There was a wonderful closeness between mother and son though and young as he was, little Nicky was very protective of her. To Lettie he was always courteous, nearly always obedient, but with his mother he showed loving care and tenderness all the time.

As for Serena — he was her whole life! Her constant battle with herself was not to spoil him, to mother him too much. She knew he was fast getting to the stage of needing a man in his life permanently.

As if following on from the thought, he told her, "Poppa phoned, Mum. He'll be here the day after tomorrow." There was no excitement, no special joy in his voice. Nicky took his father's brief, erratic appearances in his stride. He had known no other way of life.

"It's fish for supper," and this time his words were doleful. He hated fish!

"Don't worry, pet, I'll get Lettie to fix something nice for you. That goes there . . . " She reached over to fit in a piece of the puzzle, much to his annoyance; he liked to complete jigsaws without any adult help.

She found Lettie in the kitchen, busy as usual.

"Hi, Serena, feel better now?" The tall woman's keen eyes scanned her young mistress's face carefully. "You seemed a bit worried at lunchtime, pet."

"Lettie, your eyes see too much," Serena teased as she perched on the corner of the kitchen table, a slight frown creasing her brow. "It was — well, Danielle phoned me early this morning." She paused, wondering how much she should confide in Lettie.

"Did she want something?" The older woman was always wary when *that* name cropped up! In her opinion, Serena was far too soft, too gullible where her young sister was concerned. A more selfish, idle, little liar, Lettie reckoned she had yet to meet!

Serena sighed, and then on a sudden decision, told her. "She's pregnant, Lettie, wants to borrow money from me for an abortion." She saw the other's lips tighten, brown eyes snapping with anger and disgust.

"And . . . "

"I told her I didn't agree with abortion, only in exceptional cases, like rape. She — she began to argue, so I had to put her off. She's coming to see me in the morning. Oh Lettie, what am I to do?"

"I'd tell her to go and ask the father! It's his worry, not yours, my love. Here, drink this and I'll join you." She passed Serena a glass of fine sherry and then poured one for herself. "Forget it for now, supper's nearly ready."

"Oh, the fish . . . "

"It's all right, I've made a couple of

fish cakes for Nicky; he won't know there's any fish in them though!"

"Lettie, I've said it before, but what would we do without you, darling?"

Lettie put down her glass and reached out to squeeze Serena's shoulder.

"I don't intend you should find out." And with a nod in the direction of the dining-room, she turned to the stove, ready to serve their supper.

Only one end of the beautiful oval table was set, three chairs pulled out ready. The place mats and napkins were pristine white against the dark patina of the polished walnut. Good silver, cut-glass and fine china told their own tale of money well spent, no expense spared.

Serena glanced round with pleasure; she loved her home. Everything in it had been lovingly chosen in the days when she and Gino had been so happy together.

After supper they had their coffee in the long lounge with its comfortable settee and armchairs, each with its own small table at the side. Colourful prints on the walls echoed the tints in the cushions and covers. At the far end, long velvet curtains screened the French windows leading out to the conservatory and balcony.

It was out there that her love of colour had had its fling. As if to make up for the lack of a garden, she had filled tubs, urns and jardinieres with flowering shrubs and gorgeous plants. Along the side walls hung colourful baskets; trailing vines disguised pipes and posts; pots of early spring flowers lined the window ledges. She saw to it that all the year round there was bright foliage and flowers. And she was thankful that Lettie had a really green finger and didn't mind spending so much time watering and caring for the abundance of growing things out there.

On the tiled floor were plaited straw mats; the furniture was of expensive white cane, the scatter cushions bright and comfortable. They spent a lot of time out there, never tiring of the view of London and the river. Nicky told everyone he could see St Paul's from up there, whilst Lettie and Serena thanked dear Walter's forethought for the safety all around him.

They even had a television set in one corner out there too, and as the whole apartment had an efficient central-heating system, they just ignored the bad weather and used the enclosed balcony all the time. In fact, Nicky loved to be out there when the wind blew downriver and the rain lashed at the glass while he was snug and warm inside. So he never felt the lack of a garden and he had his little friends in often for tea. Whenever possible, either Lettie or Serena took him to the nearest park to play.

But for how long would all this satisfy a growing boy Serena pondered watching his face as he was engrossed in the cowboy film on the glowing screen.

And how long could she go on

living this half-life of hers? What a silly little fool she'd been to marry so young, without really knowing Gino. Looking back on her hurried wedding with no parents or friends to support her, she knew she had no one to blame but herself. Thank goodness her parents had long since forgiven her and absolutely adored their young grandson.

But whatever the outcome, she would never live with Gino as his wife again knowing he would always have other women.

"Come on, young lad, your film's done, isn't it? It's bedtime for you." Lettie bustled in, a glass of milk in her hand for Nicky. "I'm going out for a while, Serena; you'll be all right?"

"Of course. Matthew's popping in soon, so don't hurry back."

The housekeeper had her own friends: came and went to suit herself as well as Serena and Nicky. She had a quiet, discreet way of making herself scarce when it was necessary, so that when

Matthew arrived later, Serena was sitting alone, deep in thought.

"Hello, darling." She reached up to kiss his cheek, pleased as always to see him.

"All alone?"

"Yes. Nicky's in bed and Lettie's out. Can I get you a drink?"

"Yes, please." He sat down with a faint sigh of contentment. This was how he liked it — just him and the woman he loved, here alone. "Now then, tell me what was worrying you this morning. Are you going to tell me and let me help you, darling?"

With a drink in her hand, she sat beside him on the settee, wondering how to begin.

"It's Danielle . . . " she felt Matthew stiffen beside her, and before he could say anything, she went on, "She's pregnant, Matthew."

"Good lord!" He hadn't been expecting that and the disgust showed for a moment on his face. He was very old-fashioned in many things and unmarried young mothers was one of them! He waited for her to go on.

"And she wants to have an abortion; wants me to lend her the money to get it done quickly, privately."

Something in her voice made him ask, "Is that a problem? You're not short of money are you? If so . . . "

"No! No, it's not that." She paused and then in a low voice went on, "It's just that I don't believe — don't really approve of abortions, Matthew."

"Ah, that's your convent schooling, pet, I guess. But surely it's the best thing in this case, isn't it?"

Somehow Serena had expected him to agree with her. He was usually so staid, so predictable, and now she was surprised and confused.

"What does the chap say? Has she told him yet?"

"I don't know. She phoned me early this morning and it came as a shock. I — I didn't want to discuss it over the phone. When I told her I didn't agree, she started to argue loudly, so I told her I'd see her in the morning."

"And you're worried, of course?" Matthew's voice was gentle, wanting to spare her the anxiety.

"I — I can't, I can't just give her the money to kill a baby! It's not fair that she should ask me to. I'll have to tell her so, but I know she'll get angry with me. I never usually refuse her anything. But this . . . oh Matthew, why on earth wasn't she more careful?"

"If I was you, I'd give her a cheque, and then forget all about it. It's her life, her decision, my dear. Try and treat it as an ordinary loan. Or tell her to ask the man in question for the money, if you can't appease your conscience that far. You can't really refuse to help her, can you?"

"I know." Beside him, Serena stirred in her seat, her lovely face ravaged with misery. "I'll just have to wait till morning . . . "

He reached over and took her hand in his.

"I really came to see you, to talk

49

to you about us, Serena." Again he felt her tense, but went on now while his courage lasted. "You could get a divorce now, darling. It's ages ago since . . . " He paused, a slight flush staining his cheeks.

"Since I slept with Gino!" she put in succinctly, and then regretted it. Poor Matthew, he must be hating all this.

"Yes, quite. You could sue now. I'll send you to a good man, and then we could be married. You know how much I love you, Serena. Please say yes."

"I'm not sure. I don't know that I want to get married again," she said desperately.

"I don't blame you for feeling like that, but I'd take such good care of you, my love." He brought her hand up to his lips and the gentle gesture touched her as a more passionate one would not have done.

"And what about Nicky — and your mother — and my job?" she asked quietly. And deep down, she knew that if she loved him enough, all these problems could be resolved in time.

"One step at a time, darling. Start the ball rolling for your divorce; everything else will sort itself out once you're free."

There was so much to think about. She sighed and squeezed his hand fondly.

"Give me time to consider it, will you, Matthew?" she begged.

"When's Gino coming here next?" She could tell how much he hated even saying her husband's name.

"He rang Nicky today. Soon, I think."

"Then ask him — no, *tell* him, you're starting divorce proceedings. He could still see the boy."

But was Matthew hoping she would let Gino take his son for good, she wondered? No, of course not. Again she scolded herself for the thought. Being married to Gino had changed her; she no longer really trusted any man, except dear Walter.

"Please give me time to think it over;

leave it to me for now."

"Right, but I want you, Serena, soon," he said, and with that he pulled her across his lap, kissing her mouth, her eyes, her neck.

Something stirred deep down inside her. It was so long since she'd been loved. Yet she didn't know whether she wanted Matthew to be the one to bring her back to life and love. Somewhere, between Gino's quick flares of passion and Matthew's gentle, sedate lovemaking, there had to be something, someone. She knew now that she had yet to reach that high peak, that true depth of love.

But would that eventually be reached with Matthew? She doubted it, and twenty-six was still far too young to settle again for something less. Matthew seemed quite satisfied with her response and she was fond of him. But was this enough?

He had just left when Lettie returned.

"Well, pet, had a nice evening?" Her smiling eyes took in the sight of the crumpled settee cushions and she grinned widely.

"As I've said before, my dear Lettie, your eyes see too much! I'm off to bed. Lock up, will you? 'Night."

Lettie put her hand on Serena's arm, detaining her.

"I just want you to be happy; want what's best for you and young Nicky." The warm sincerity in her words brought a gleam of moisture to the younger woman's eyes.

"I know you do, Lettie. Bless you."

* * *

Serena tossed and turned most of the night away. How could she sleep when she had so much on her mind? She hated the thought of a quarrel with Danielle; she might even take her request for money to their parents and Serena didn't want that to happen.

She dreaded too telling Gino that she was going to put in for a divorce, but about that, her mind was definitely made up. Whether she married Matthew or not, she was too young to be tied to a loveless, empty marriage any longer. After all, whether they married or not, she and Matthew could spend more time together. Why should she send him home every night and spend the rest of the evening alone?

But what of Nicky? Oh God, what a mess! She thumped her pillow and for once indulged in self-pity. She was still only a young woman . . .

* * *

The next morning, she looked tired and wan; still undecided and worried about Danielle's problem. Walter, as usual, was quick to notice the dark shadows beneath her eyes.

"You need a holiday, my dear."

"I'm all right, you old fusspot. Just a bit restless last night, that's all. Touch of spring I reckon."

He knew better than to pursue it any

further, so changed the subject.

"That reminds me, Serena, it's time we started considering the Champagne — soon be the wedding season. Let me have the latest lists of *le grands vins*, will you?" And they were soon busy with the morning's work, only to be interrupted by Danielle.

Walter rose. "Almost coffee time. I'll see you later. 'Bye for now, Danielle." As courteous as ever, he left them together and went downstairs.

"Well, Serena, made up your mind?" The young girl's voice held a touch of bravado that didn't quite deceive her older sister who watched her closely for a moment.

As usual, Danielle was dressed in the latest clothes, all chosen to enhance her voluptuous figure. Her hair was a deeper shade of blonde than Serena's; her features not so fine. In fact, there was already a look of dissipation about the younger girl. And she knew it, and felt a deep envy that Serena, married and with a son of seven, could still

55

retain her air of innocence.

Crossing her long legs in the tight skirt, she returned her sister's gaze with a brazen stare.

"As I told you on the phone, Danielle, I don't believe in abortion, only in certain cases."

"Oh, don't be such a drag! Anyone would think you were sixty instead of twenty-six. Everybody does it. What would I do with a little kid?"

"What does the father say?" Serena put in quietly.

"I haven't told him. He — he wouldn't agree," Danielle answered sullenly.

"Well, then . . . "

"He's a Catholic, that's why. I can't even ask him for the money."

"Why should I give it to you then, Danielle? When it's against my principles too?" Serena asked pointedly.

At that, her sister rose from her seat, her face livid with anger.

"Why you? You mealy-mouthed fool,

why you? I'll tell you why." The anger boiled over and Serena shrank back in her chair in dismay. "Because it's Gino's kid, that's why! Yes, your husband's! Does that make me one of the special cases you'd agree to, does it?"

The colour drained from Serena's face; shock wide in her blue eyes and she suddenly felt sick.

"Gino's? Oh no, I don't believe you!"

"Ask him! Ask him how often we've slept together, dear Serena. He won't deny it — he never does. But he's already chucked me over, for a redhead this time." Danielle's voice cracked, bitter anger almost choking her. Sorry for herself but with none for the pale-faced sister looking at her in disbelief.

"You know what the Italians are like about kids; he'd never agree to me getting rid of one of his, or give me the money, so you'd better change your mind pretty quickly, Sister dear."

"Oh God!" Serena buried her face

in her hands, her head spinning. What should she do now? She took a deep breath, trying to still the pounding of her heart.

Suddenly, Danielle reached over and touched her shoulder.

"Please, Serena, you've got to help me. I'm sorry, but you and Gino haven't lived as man and wife for years, have you? I didn't mean to hurt you, but you're the only one I can turn to now." Gone was the brash bravado, and suddenly Serena was remembering all the times she had shielded her little sister in the past. Was it partly *her* fault that Gino turned to other women?

With a deep sigh, she reached for her cheque book.

"Very well, but please, don't tell me anything more about this." Her hand trembled as she wrote out the cheque, her heart as heavy as lead.

With obvious relief, Danielle took it and put it in her bag.

"Thanks, Sis. Lord knows when I'll pay this back . . . "

"Don't bother! It's Gino's responsibility and it's his money." Even as she spoke, she still felt sick at having to go against her own beliefs. "Don't let Mum and Dad know about all this, will you?"

"Of course not. I'll go now — thanks again, Serena."

For a few minutes after she'd gone, Serena sat there staring into space, and then finally went downstairs to help Walter check the lists of Champagnes, thankful for the job that kept her busy.

★ ★ ★

"I've made you a picture, Mum. Do you like it?" Giving him a hug, putting behind her the cares of the day, she looked fondly at the childish drawing. "That's you and that's Lettie and those are all the new plants, see?"

"I've told him I'm not as fat as that," Lettie put in, her eyes twinkling. "More like Picasso than Michelangelo, I'd say, wouldn't you, Serena?"

"It's lovely. Where shall we put it, Nicky?"

"In your room, so's you can see it all the time."

"Of course, where else?" Serena laughed. "Thanks, pet."

Once he was settled in front of the television, the two women were able to talk in the kitchen.

"I gave Danielle the money, Lettie."

"You changed your mind then, pet?" Something in the girl's voice told Lettie that there was more involved, but she wisely didn't ask.

"Yes, I had to; there was more to it."

As Serena's words faltered, Lettie put in quietly, "I'm sure there was. You did right; you had to help your sister. Now forget all about it. We'll dish up the meal, shall we?"

Over the food, they listened to Nicky's chatter about his day. Thank heavens he was happy at his little day school, thought Serena.

"I fished this note out of the washing

machine, Serena. As far as I can read, it's about a coffee morning next week at the school. Want me to go for you, pet? I'll make some cakes and so on."

"Will you? Good; we're a bit busy just now downstairs."

"Look, Mum! Look, that's Poppa's car . . . " But even as they turned to Nicky and the television, the news reader was finishing the report.

" . . . a six car pile-up on the M25. There is no news yet of casualties." And the picture had changed to the next news item.

"It was Poppa's car, I saw the number plate," Nicky insisted. He hadn't fully realized what was involved, of course.

White-faced, Serena looked across at Lettie, who shook her head warningly.

"It couldn't be, could it . . . ?"

"I doubt if he could see any special car in that pile-up, love. Don't worry, I'm sure he was wrong," Lettie murmured.

"Perhaps there'll be more on the ten

o'clock news. Do you think I should ring . . . ?"

"No!" Lettie put in sharply. "Wait; you'll hear soon enough. You can't go on a child's glimpse of a picture, can you?"

Worried sick, Serena waited anxiously as the time dragged slowly. She bathed Nicky, trying to hide her fears as he splashed happily around. Reading him a bedtime story, she kept glancing at her watch.

"Any phone call, Lettie?"

"No, love. And you know what they say about no news." Even Lettie's face showed the strain and by ten o'clock they both sat waiting for Big Ben to strike, both pairs of eyes watching the screen intently.

" . . . there are three people killed and several severely injured." The careful newscaster's voice was quietly unconcerned. "No details are being given until next of kin have been informed."

"Oh God," Serena moaned.

"Here, drink this." Lettie held out a glass with a small amount of brandy in it. Serena gagged, and then forced it down. Her face was pinched with pallor and her hands shook. Lettie's eyes were full of pity for her; it was the waiting that was always the worst!

It was nearly midnight when they came to tell her; a young policeman and a policewoman, standing there, white-faced, hating their job. Serena's mind was numb with shock, knowing pity for the two young people in front of her, sorry that they had this awful task to do.

Finally, it began to sink in — Gino was dead! Smashed almost beyond recognition in that terrible mêlée — he and the red-haired young girl in the fast car with him!

She sat slumped in the chair, trying to think, to take in what had happened. A few minutes later, Lettie took the police through to the lift, talking quietly, listening to their instructions, knowing she had to be strong for her young employer's sake.

What a tragedy, such a waste of life. And poor Serena and Nicky . . . dear God, help them, she prayed silently.

"Try to lie down, pet. There's nothing we can do till morning."

Wide-eyed, deathly cold, Serena lay looking up at the ceiling, seeing pictures there. Pictures of the early days, of a loving Gino; remembering how it was when passion had died. Such a waste of her young years, and now of Gino's life.

Gradually, thinking of him, so handsome, so full of life, the tears began to flow down her cheeks. Sorrow swamped her then for the tragic way it had all ended.

She wondered, too, about the young girl who had died in the crash with him. Even to the end, Gino had run true to form, with yet another beautiful female beside him. Now his widow was left to grieve, full of regrets for the waste . . . all the waste. Wondering what she could say to their little son?

* * *

Two days later, Lettie went with her to the tiny chapel of rest belonging to the nearby Catholic church. It was so quiet in there and their footsteps sounded loud as they approached the coffin lying on trestles in the shadow of the statue of a gentle-eyed Madonna. Because of the terrible injuries, the coffin lid had been closed after the post mortem.

Dry-eyed now, tense with the effort of keeping calm, Serena laid a spray of rosebuds on the lid; bowed her head for a while in prayer, and then a final farewell to the man who had been her husband in reality for such a short time, who had given her a beloved son, some sweet memories and so many bitter ones.

"Ciao, Gino, mio caro." She kissed her fingertips and then pressed them for a second to the coffin in farewell. Farewell to a part of her life . . .

That afternoon, she went to collect

Nicky herself from school. Her heart lurched with loving pride as she watched him come tumbling through the school gates, black curls bouncing, his dark eyes lighting with pleasure when he saw her standing there.

"Hi, Mum! Can we go for an ice-cream before we go home? And can my friend, Tim, come too?"

"Not today, darling," her bottom lip trembled. "I — I have something to talk about — just we two."

"Oh." She saw the brightness fade from his eyes. "Are you poorly?" he asked.

"No, I'm fine, pet." But Nicky was still not assured.

"Is Poppa home yet?" Serena swallowed convulsively, trying to clear the tight lump in her throat.

"No, Nicky. Is this your ice-cream shop?" He nodded, still not convinced that his mother was all right.

They chose their ice-creams and took them to a quiet corner and sat down at the plastic-topped table. Nicky took a spoonful of ice-cream, watching her face from beneath his long black eyelashes. At that moment, he looked so like Gino she wanted to cry out, to refute what she must tell him.

He had to know, but how do you explain to a seven year old about death? Hands clenched beneath the table, she found herself praying for the right words.

"Nicky," she began quietly, "you remember seeing a picture on the television of Poppa's car in the crash?"

The dark lashes blinked suddenly, and then revealed equally dark eyes now clouded with alarm.

"Yes, it *was* Poppa's car. And now he won't be coming home to see us — ever. Oh Nicky, my darling . . . " She reached out and clasped his small hand.

The little boy gave a convulsive shudder and then slowly, two big tears crept down his cheeks and his lips quivered.

"He's dead? Poppa's dead?"

"Yes, darling. He was badly hurt. So badly, he fell asleep and didn't wake up again. Do you understand what I'm telling you, Nicky?"

He nodded numbly and the tears continued to fall.

"A boy in my class — his poppa died in the crash. He cried in school." He swallowed hard and bit his trembling lip. "I won't cry in school, Mum. I'll look after you." And then, as if on a sudden terrible thought, he asked fearfully, "You won't die, will you, or I'd only have Lettie?"

"No, my darling, I'm not going to leave you. We'll be together, you and I and Lettie always. Just like we are when Poppa's away — only this time he — he won't be coming home to see us."

Nicky moved his head from side to side as if trying to accept what she was saying. As he rubbed away his tears with one chubby knuckle, the misery in Serena's throat almost choked her. Dear heaven, if only she could spare him this grief; he was so little . . .

"It'll be quite all right if you cry at home, pet — to cry sometimes when you remember your father. We both will, but we'll have to love and comfort each other, won't we?" She reached up to her throat trying to move the lump threatening to choke her. Again those big dark eyes sought hers as he nodded. Then with a tightening of his lips, he squared his young shoulders in an almost adult gesture, pushed aside his dish of ice-cream and rose to go.

"Let's go home, Mum." Then, forgetting to be grown-up, he put his hand in hers, seeking comfort, giving comfort. And as they walked along the street, Serena passed through her own private little hell, knowing how her young son was feeling, and not being able to help him come to terms with his loss.

Taking his blazer and schoolbag, Lettie glanced across at Serena, who read the message in her eyes and nodded to let her know she had told Nicky the sad news. For once he didn't rush across to the television, but Serena was thankful to see he ate a little at teatime. Sitting down on the rug, he reached for his jigsaw puzzle.

"I want to get this finished before Poppa comes . . . " he began, then painfully remembered that Gino wouldn't be coming to see the new game he had bought. Tears welled up once more as he stumbled to his feet as he dashed out to his room.

As Serena made to follow him, Lettie reached out to stop her, murmuring softly, "Leave him, love. Let him have his grieving time — alone. He'll be all right, you'll see."

"Oh, but Lettie . . . "

"I know just how you're feeling, but he has to come to terms with this himself, Serena, young as he is."

Of course, Lettie was right. All the same, when she had tucked him up in his little bed, she read to him for a long time and didn't leave him until he was fast asleep.

Half an hour later, they were surprised

to hear the soft whirr of the lift, followed by the doorbell ringing.

"I'll go." Lettie rose and hurried into the hall. There was the low murmur of her voice and then the sound of a deeper one. Serena looked up to see a strange look on Lettie's face.

"There's someone to see you, Serena. I'll — er — be in my room, dear, if you need me." And as she went away, Serena rose to see the tall figure of a man coming into the lounge. For a moment, the room seemed to whirl round and she almost fainted with shock. For a split second there, she had thought it was Gino!

Her knees felt so weak, she slumped back into the chair, her heart thumping like a mad thing inside her.

"I am Roberto — Roberto Ercoli." The voice sounded like Gino's, with the same Latin accent, but with something else . . . it had a hard, severe note that made her suddenly go cold.

"Of course you are," she managed. "You're Gino's elder brother. The family resemblance is all too obvious. I'm Serena Ercoli, his wife." Her words faltered. "His widow."

She held out a shaking hand, but whether the tall, dark-haired man saw it or not, he didn't take it and she let it fall to her side.

"Please — sit down, Roberto. Can I get you a drink?"

"No, *grazie*." Again his voice was cold, but he sat down facing her. "We — I did not know *mio fratello* — Gino had a wife."

Once more the walls seemed to sway around her as the shock hit her. Shock — cold like a block of ice inside her, made her stare at him in bewilderment.

"I don't believe you!" she gasped. "We've been married for over eight years." As she drew in a deep breath, struggling for composure, she stared at the man opposite her. Never again would she mistake him for Gino! This man's face was cast in a much stronger mould.

His dark eyes were hard; his chin was firmer and clear cut, as were his sharply drawn cheekbones. Like Gino and Nicky, he had the same beautiful long eyelashes. His skin was tanned to a dark gold, his nose straight and proud. But it was his mouth that caught the eye. It was sensuously shaped, expressive, with the edges well defined. For one absurd moment Serena wondered what a kiss from those lips would be like.

"Gino always told me — you didn't want to see me. He told me he'd tried to persuade you all to come to terms with our marriage."

With an expressive shrug, he said, "I only had word of you from the London office. I've come to take my brother's body back for burial. My father is not well enough to travel, and my mother will not leave him. The shock of his death has devastated them both — all of us."

To think that all those years, Gino had been lying to her!

"I can't believe it. It's so hard to

take in that all this time I've been thinking so badly about them. But they didn't know! And Nicky — they don't know that they have such a dear little grandson."

Suddenly it was all too much, and she began to cry bitterly, the tears streaming unchecked down her face.

The man's lips tightened; he didn't intend to be taken in by this woman's tears. With a cynical glance round, he said coldly, "You've certainly not lacked for money it seems, *signora*. My brother was a fine catch, *si*?" She drew in a deep shuddering breath, trying to control the anger the man's words aroused.

"I work, Roberto. I have always worked! I earn enough to keep myself and my son. All this — " with an angry jerk of her arm she indicated the sumptuously furnished room — "All this, was Gino's wish, not mine. I didn't marry for money. I loved Gino deeply when we married."

If the meaning behind her last words

was clear to him, Roberto Ercoli didn't disclose it.

"I will have that drink you offered, please." Without asking his preference, Serena crossed to the walnut cabinet and poured him a glass of red Italian wine, and as she passed it to him, the light intensed its rich ruby glow.

To her disgust, the touch of his fingers sent a quick tremor along the whole length of her arm. There was something very attractive about him — attractive and dangerous, so that she was fascinated and frightened at the same time.

He took a sip of the wine and then looked down into the glass.

"One of ours, I see."

"A Bardolino?" Her eyebrows rose. "I didn't know." It sounded false even to her own ears. "Gino never spoke much at all about the Ercoli vineyards, or his family, or anything." Slight hysteria made her words shrill. "He always got angry if I persisted . . . "

His glance registered his contempt as

he sneered, "And you did not know that there is much wealth in the Ercoli family; wealth that your son will now share?"

Her face was flushed as she answered him heatedly. "I know Gino was never short of money; I thought he earned it. He was so very rarely at home here."

How dare he come here and speak to her as if she was some . . . some floozie who had only married his younger brother for his money!

"You fell out of love with him?"

She gazed at his face intently. He was a stranger and she wasn't used to opening her heart to strangers. But his cold, contemptuous manner was making her burn with anger.

"From the day our son was born, I refused to share his bed, Roberto." The words dropped coldly like hard pebbles between them.

"Perchè? Why?" Once more those supercilious eyebrows rose in query.

"Because too many other girls shared

it, that's why," she stormed. "And anyway, he'd grown tired of me by then. He usually grew tired of his women after they'd slept a few times with him."

"I find all this difficult to believe, *Signora.*"

"As I do that you all knew nothing of Gino's wife and child!" Serena's shoulders straightened, her lips firm, her voice proud. In no manner was this haughty Italian going to have it all his own way. In spite of the powerful attraction he exuded even at a distance, she would not be intimidated by him, she told herself angrily.

Again came that so-Latin shrug. After a moment, he suggested, "You will come to Italy for the funeral?"

"No." She paused and then added softly, "I have said my farewell to Gino and I'm quite prepared for you to take him home with you." The tears stung hotly behind her eyes, and she struggled to blink them away. "Nicky needs me here. I can't leave him and he's far too young to attend a funeral Mass."

"Very well, *signora*." He rose, towering above her and she was suddenly aware of the aroma of his aftershave. That, and something else — almost animal-like. "I will keep you informed of any future developments shall I?"

"I don't want anything I am not entitled to, Roberto, please remember that. But my son is part of your family whether you like it or not."

There was a definite smile on his lips at that, but it was grim and failed quite noticeably to reach his dark eyes as he stood staring down at her.

"Your son is an heir; we will not forget that. May I see him, *suo figlio*?"

For a moment she wanted to refuse, but something in his voice made her agree.

3

"**V**ERY well, come with me." Stiff-backed, Serena led the way to the little boy's bedroom. It had every comfort possible, with its walls lined with nursery-tale posters, its small red table and chairs, shelves of toys and books.

As usual, he had thrown off his cover and a round bare bottom was showing out of his figured pyjamas. His dark hair showed even darker against the white of the pillow; black eyelashes fanned out on chubby cheeks.

As he leaned over the bed, she heard Roberto catch his breath.

"*Bello ragazzo*, so like Gino." There was a hint of surprise in the husky words. Again Serena's anger rose. What was he expecting? Of course Nicky was like his father!

In spite of her resentment, she

watched closely as he reached out and gently, carefully pushed back a strand of the dark silky hair.

"He is very beautiful, your little one. How his grandparents will love him." The tenderness in his voice filled her with confusion. Was there two sides to this arrogant man?

"He must now live in Italy, learn to understand what being a member of the Casa d'Ercoli means." The cold, haughty manner was back again as he turned to her, his voice low so as not to disturb the sleeping child.

"Nicky stays with me!" she burst out possessively. "I am his mother and I'll never give him up, never!" White-hot temper made her stalk back into the lounge, leaving him to follow.

"We shall see, *signora*." His voice was cold with contempt. "You will be hearing from me soon. *Addio*." And over his shoulder he called a soft, "*Ciao, piccolo mio*" in the direction of Nicky's bedroom.

At the door to the lift, Serena

said coldly, "Goodbye, Roberto." The finality of her farewell made it clear she didn't want to see him again.

Her calm deserted her the moment the lift door closed, and her heart was heavy as she went along to Lettie's room to tell her what had happened.

"I just can't believe that Gino *never* told his family about our marriage — about Nicky, Lettie. He just kept putting me off every time I mentioned it to him."

"He lied, Serena, my love," the housekeeper said baldly. "Right from the start, he lied — to you and to them."

"I've been a naive fool. I should have suspected — insisted on knowing more, Lettie." Her voice was bitter at her own stupidity. "But somehow Italy seemed far away and our brief times together too short to spend in arguments." Her throat thickened with misery and disgust at herself, but as she and Gino had grown apart, she'd been no longer interested or concerned that her in-laws had never contacted or acknowledged her.

Now this . . . this hard-faced elder brother wanted her son to live in Italy with the rest of the Ercoli family. Never! she vowed vehemently. Thoughts of losing her precious son made her heart freeze like a block of ice inside her.

"Stop worrying, pet. They can't take him away from you. And you don't need their money or their influence. But they should pay towards Nicky's upkeep, his education later on," Lettie pointed out sensibly. "But for now — forget it. Put it all behind you now, Serena. Think about Matthew; he loves you, I know. And he'll make you a far better husband than . . . " Remembering that she was about to speak ill of the dead, she closed her lips tightly.

"Oh Lettie, don't ever leave us." Serena gulped away the lump in her throat, trying to forget the last half-hour. "We must give Nicky a lot of extra loving, mustn't we? He's sure to miss his papa."

"Only for a while. A child's memory is very short; he'll soon stop grieving. After all, it isn't as if he ever saw much of his father, is it?" And if Lettie's words sounded a little callous, she couldn't help it. She'd never had much time for a chap who slept around as Gino had done. And him with a lovely wife like Serena!

In her opinion it wasn't natural that such a young girl should have to live like a nun. She told herself right then that the next time Matthew came to dinner, she would absent herself for the whole night. It was about time their romance moved on a bit!

For the next few days, Serena seemed to be living and working in a haze. She tried to spend more time with Nicky; met him from school; took him and his little friend for tea or burgers at a lively cafe nearby. He didn't appear to be thinking of his father and she and Lettie thought he was forgetting his death.

Until one night, Serena awoke and lay staring into the dark, wondering what had awakened her. And then she heard it again — a child's cry. Nicky! Hurriedly she scrambled out of bed and ran along to his room.

In the low light she saw his flushed face, his hair tousled as he tossed on the pillow. His cheeks were streaked with tears as he sobbed, —

"Papa, Papa! I want my papa . . . "

At the sight of her son's distress, Serena's heart twisted and she gathered him close, nestling the dark head to her breast, crooning softly, "Hush, *bambino*, hush. Mummy's here, my darling." She watched as he struggled to remember. "You were crying in your sleep, Nicky." Small fists knuckled away the tears, his soft lips trembling.

"I don't want Papa to be dead. I want him to come home."

"I know, sweetheart, but he can't. That horrid car smash . . . you remember?"

He sighed, and the sound wrenched her heart again. If only she could bear his pain for him. Nodding, he snuggled closer, sniffing away further tears.

"Yes — I remember now."

"Would you like to come into my bed, darling?" Again the nod of that dark head and she lifted him and carried him through to her bedroom.

Long after he'd gone to sleep, she lay staring wide-eyed into the darkness, her whole being aching for her child's pain, his loss.

The only news she had from Roberto Ercoli was a heavily embossed, black-edged card announcing a funeral mass in Italy for her husband. As she translated it, hot tears splashed down blotting out some of the words.

She and Lettie tried to fill Nicky's days so that he had little time to grieve, and gradually, as all small children do, he seemed to forget. Only occasionally would he mention his papa, and when he did, it was calmly, without distress.

Matthew was showing a thoughtful understanding as she refused to leave Nicky to go out with him. But Serena knew he was getting tired of being rejected however lovingly she did it. "If only he got on with small children a little better, Lettie," she murmured, gazing down at her laced fingers weeks later.

"Don't worry, love. Wait till he gets one of his own."

"I'm not sure. I wish I could think that way. But I must put Nicky's well-being first, before my own, Lettie."

The older woman folded the small T-shirt she had just ironed, her eyes thoughtful.

"I think Nicky's all right now. Why not leave him with me and have a night out. Y'know, pet, you can't keep refusing Matthew; no man likes to be put off all the time."

Serena shrugged. "I'll see."

But that afternoon when Matthew rang, she agreed to go out for a meal with him that evening.

"You look beautiful, my love. It seems ages since I had you to myself." The black dress made her hair look fairer, and in the shaded light from the little lamp on their table her skin looked almost translucent. As usual, Matthew had chosen a quiet, elegant restaurant where the service was discreet, the food excellent.

"I know, Matthew; you've been an angel, but for a while I had to give Nicky all my time and loving. He's such a little boy to lose his father," she finished gently.

"He didn't see Gino all that often." By the stubborn tightening of his lips, she could see he wanted to say more, so she reached across and placed her hand over his.

"I'm here now, darling. And I mean to put Gino and all I've gone through these last few years behind me."

His face brightened and he squeezed her hand warmly.

"Good, perhaps now you'll think of marrying me."

Startled, without thinking, she pulled her hand away. "No," she muttered. "Please — don't ask me. It's too soon; I'm not ready." She almost told him that she wasn't sure that she loved him, but she bit her lip and swallowed hard. "Let's spend more time together."

Hopefully he looked into her face. "Just you and I?" Matthew's thick brows rose in query.

Again she felt the touch of doubt inside her, but as she had refused him so often lately, she nodded.

"Just you and I, Matthew, yes. Lettie will always have Nicky for me."

"Good," he paused, a pensive look on his face. And then, as if making up his mind, he went on, "You're free now, Serena. Free and young enough to want to be loved. I've waited . . . " Again he paused, and then, his voice persuasive, he said, "What about coming away with me this weekend, just you and I together?"

And as he emphasized the last words, she understood just what his invitation implied. A heated refusal rose to her lips, and then she saw the entreaty in his brown eyes. She couldn't refuse yet again!

Later that evening, in a shadowy lane in the darkness of his car, his kisses made her glad she hadn't refused. Her body began to tell her just how much she needed a man. She'd been celibate far too long, and after all, she was free now.

When she was in his arms, felt his need, the fervour of his kisses, her whole body responded. She felt a burning heat somewhere deep down. She was still young and had no need to feel ashamed of nature's urges, she told herself.

But did she love Matthew? Enough to sleep with him, to commit herself to him for the rest of her life? And she knew that this time it had to be just that. This time she must not make the same mistake again. And what of Nicky? Could she present him with a new father? No — it was too soon! But could she keep refusing Matthew?

Long after she had undressed and

got into bed, she tossed and turned. Memories of the early days of her love for Gino kept coming back unbidden. She had been almost a child then; now she was older with a little boy's welfare to put before her own. Sighing deeply, she pummelled the pillow restlessly. She had agreed to spend a weekend with Matthew at a quiet little bay on the Sussex coast.

The next morning, the dark shadows beneath her lovely eyes told their own tale of a sleepless night. And she walked back from taking Nicky to his junior school still wondering if she'd done right.

"What do you think, Lettie?" The pale spring sunshine lit the kitchen although it was still cold outside, and the older woman cupped the hot mug of coffee in her hands watching Serena's worried frown.

"You go, love. It'll do you good. My sister's grandchildren are there for the weekend, so I'll take Nicky along. He'll have a great time, you'll see."

Serena shifted in her seat. "Oh, I know I can leave him with you, Lettie. But I don't think . . . I'm not sure I'm ready to sleep with Matthew. And that's what this weekend means."

"He doesn't turn you on?"

Lettie's blunt question brought a faint smile to Serena's face, as she answered, "Yes, of course he does." Her face flushed as she added, "But I've never slept around."

"Then it's high time you did for once," Lettie told her firmly. "You're free now, to do whatever you want to do. Besides," she finished, "Matthew's been very patient."

* * *

It was a bit warmer that following Friday morning when Matthew picked her up. The flower beds were bright with early daffodils and tulips, the almond blossom was powdering the trees with pink. And in spite of her misgivings, Serena felt her spirits rise. Nicky had been excited at going away with Lettie and had packed and unpacked his rucksack several times, unable to decide which toys to take with him. Apart from a hurried kiss, he had been too busy to worry about his mother's departure. And a quick pang of dismay made her realize that he was growing up fast!

It was a pleasant run to the coast; their hotel was small but comfortable, with a few early guests and several regulars. Watching Matthew sign the register and accept the key, her face burned. How stupid, she told herself, so many unmarried couples came away together these days, didn't they? All the same she felt the hint of constraint as they took the old-fashioned lift up to the second floor.

Matthew had booked a suite; two bedrooms with a bathroom between them. With her eyes avoiding the sight of the king-sized bed, she went over to the dressing-table and pretended to straighten her hair. As she did, through the mirror, she saw Matthew watching her, a look on his face that was unreadable. She felt her heart pounding, her breath tight in her throat as she stood quietly waiting. And, as he slipped his arms around her waist, she leaned back against his strong body, thrilling to the touch of his lips on the curve of her neck.

"If you knew how long I've wanted this, my darling — to have you all to myself." His lips followed the gentle line of her neck and she felt his warm breath stir the pulse beating there. She turned in his arms, reaching up to clasp her hands behind his neck, holding close to him. She covered his chin with quick passionate little kisses, and as she did, she could feel the deep heavy thud of his heartbeat against her breast.

"You'd better let me unpack my things, Matthew, it'll soon be lunchtime." His reluctance to release her was all too obvious, but some hesitation deep inside her made her want to put off his love-making.

The half-timbered dining-room with its heavy Jacobean furniture was quiet and peaceful with the early spring sunshine casting bright patterns through the diamond-paned windows. As the waitress showed them to a corner table, she was pleased to see that the other diners took no notice of them. It was the first time she had stayed at a hotel with anyone else but Gino. There had been a couple of swift tentative affairs since they had parted, but something had held her back from complete fulfilment. The fear of making the same mistake again; the loathing of being thought promiscuous, of despising herself for giving herself to a man she didn't really love . . .

"I'll order a Riesling, shall I, darling?" She nodded and silently blessed him for not choosing an Italian wine. For this weekend, she wanted to forget, to put behind her the last years that had been such a waste. A waste except for Nicky . . . and with that thought there followed another — was he all right, was he missing her, fretting for Gino?

Matthew looked up and saw the pensive shadow that passed over her lovely face. He reached out to touch her hand, and quickly she dismissed her thoughts to concentrate on the dear man who was expecting so much from this weekend.

"Let's go for a nice long walk after lunch, shall we? It's ages since I took a decent stroll." And if he had wanted to do something else, he didn't let her know it, and agreed with a smile.

"Me, too. We'll pick up a map at the desk. Now what shall we order?"

The food was excellent but very filling and they were both glad to walk off its effect when they had finally finished their coffee in the little red-plush lounge.

The air was still keen with little warmth yet from the sun, so she wrapped up in a wool trouser suit of deep lilac, with a polo-necked sweater underneath and a big throw around scarf to match. The colours brought out the violet in her blue eyes, and the silver hair caught the glint of the pale sun. To the besotted man beside her, she had never looked more lovely, more desirable.

They left the little village behind and found the path leading round the bay. Small fishing boats rocked gently in the tiny harbour and out at sea one or two hardy sailors were enjoying the breeze that filled their sails. Later, away from the harbour, they climbed slowly uphill. At the top, they paused and finding a huge flat rock, they were both glad of a breather.

"Phew!" Matthew unzipped his anorak, lifting his face to the sky. "I'm out of condition — or getting old."

"Not you . . . " she began, and then something made her pause.

"I mean it though, Serena. It's time I settled down again; started a family of my own." He turned to face her, his voice serious. "What about it, darling? Have I waited long enough for your answer?"

To Serena, the sun seemed to disappear, the peaceful joy of the day fell away and all her doubts came flooding back. How she hated hurting him, but . . .

"It's too soon, Matthew."

Putting an arm round her slim shoulders, he pulled her close, his eyes solemn.

"I know. I don't mind waiting a few more months, but you know what I mean, darling." His voice pleaded. "I want to know — are you going to marry me?"

A lump rose in her throat and she moved her head from side to side in despair.

"I don't know, Matthew. Honestly I really don't know if I really love you, truly love you, or not. Enough to risk marrying again, I mean." Her blue eyes pleaded with him to understand. How could she explain?

To tell him that she was longing for something deeper. Would she know if that something came along? She was very fond of him, but some instinct told her that it wasn't enough. She couldn't face the rest of her life settling for second best, could she?

With a sudden jerk, he pulled her across his lap and placed his lips on hers with an abrupt roughness that wasn't like him at all! Perhaps it was her refusal or his disappointment, but whatever it was, it seemed as if he had lost his usual calm control. His mouth was hard on hers, and for a brief moment she struggled to pull herself from the fierce embrace.

"Are you just stringing me along, Serena? Were you just using your marriage as an excuse for not making up your mind?"

"No!" she gasped. "I've never pretended to be in love with you. Please, Matthew, you're hurting me . . . " She struggled to get free, but he held her tightly, his face flushed and angry.

"You've never let me make love with you! You can't tell me you've been celibate all the years since you and Gino split up?"

His voice was coarse and ugly as he ranted on, using words she'd never heard from him before; accusing her of horrible things.

"Don't tell me there's not been others," he raved and she really began to be afraid. And after her fear, came anger . . .

"That's my business, Matthew. But I've never been one to sleep around. I married Gino when I was far too young and innocent, but I'm not going to start experimenting now! I've far too much respect for myself and I've got my little son to consider too."

With a swift hard push, she freed herself from his strong arms and stood up, her breast heaving, the pinched pallor of fear still showing round her lips. Drawing a deep breath, she said brokenly, "I'm sorry, Matthew. More sorry than I can ever tell you. I never pretended to love you; never promised to marry you. I — I did hope that would come along, but it hasn't. And now I don't think it ever will!"

The sight of the bleak look that settled on his face at that made the tears sting behind her eyelids. She reached out a trembling hand and touched him gently.

"I'm sorry, truly sorry . . . " He shook his head numbly, pulling away from her touch.

"No, I should apologize — I came on too strong; said awful things. I'm sorry." His voice was husky with remorse, and Serena felt the tears overflow.

It was the end, wasn't it? The end of such a wonderful friendship, but she knew they couldn't go on now — it was finished. And with that thought came one of remorse and self-disgust. Perhaps she had been guilty of using Matthew and his caring love?

"I think I'd better go home. It's — it's no use . . . "

He turned and looked deeply into her eyes.

"I still love you, Serena, and if you ever change your mind . . . "

"No! No, please, don't go on waiting. Love can't be forced. I did hope it would grow, but it didn't. And it's not fair to keep you hoping and waiting any longer."

She swallowed against the solid lump in her throat and turned to gaze downhill, but it was all hazy with the tears. In her ears, she could still hear the ugly accusations he had made in his anger.

They made their way silently downhill; each wrestling with their thoughts. As they grew near to the hotel, Matthew suggested, "We'll stay over the one night. Don't worry, I won't bother you," he said bitterly. "But it will look funny if we just up and went without staying even one night. After all, there's two rooms."

Dismayed, Serena saw his lips curl in a sneer.

"Very well," she said. "I'll have dinner in my room if you don't mind."

The next morning, Serena dressed to go home, packed her overnight bag and went down to the little dining-room for late breakfast. Matthew was already seated at their corner table, a half-empty cup of coffee and a newspaper before him.

He rose quietly, his face pale beneath his tan, his expression remote.

"Good morning, Serena. Did you sleep well?" Wondering if this was sarcasm or genuine concern, she shook her head.

"Not very — and you?"

He shook out his paper, avoiding looking at her.

"Shall we say — it was a long night? Are you ready to leave after breakfast?"

"Yes," she murmured and then turned to ask for fresh coffee and a croissant as the young waitress came for her order.

It was an awkward journey back to London; the constraint between them almost a solid thing. Neither saw the beauty of the burgeoning trees, the primroses in the hedges, the brightness of the early sun.

"Do you want to stop somewhere for coffee?" Matthew broke the long silence.

"I'd rather not, thanks. I'd like to get home."

Oh God, she thought, we're like two polite strangers, both wanting this awful journey to end.

"I've been thinking, Serena, I'll go up to Edinburgh. We've been considering buying in to a firm up there."

He paused as he overtook a lorry in front, and then went on, "One of the other partners agreed to go — I wanted to stay in London with you. But now — well, I think I'll go instead. Get away — there's nothing to keep me down here."

Unhappy at the way she had upset his settled life, she asked, "What about your mother?" He shrugged as if it was no problem, and yet she knew his mother had a great influence on what he did, and always would have!

"She might like to go up north with me. We have relatives in Perth."

"Oh good." It didn't sound as if he would miss her for long, she mused bitterly, and then chided herself for the thought. He would miss her, every bit as much as she would miss him.

★ ★ ★

Without Nicky and Lettie there, the apartment seemed so quiet and empty. She put away her few clothes and then made an omelette for her lunch. But as she brought the plate to the kitchen table, her throat closed tightly and she knew she wouldn't be able to swallow any food. So with a mug of coffee in hand, she scanned the Sunday papers, hoping Nicky was enjoying himself with Lettie's young relations.

And he certainly had. He was bursting with news when he and Lettie came in about six o'clock.

It had seemed a long and lonely

104

afternoon for Serena with the miserable thoughts; the pangs of regret and remorse she had been feeling about the ending of her friendship with Matthew. And it had left its mark on her face.

But she tried to put it all aside as she listened to her young son's chatter.

"We made some toffee, Mum. Look, I've brought you a bit to taste. Go on, try it, it's lovely." To please him, she put a small lump of the sticky sweet into her mouth as he watched her anxiously with those dark eyes of his.

"M'mm, yes, it is nice. Can I save this till tomorrow?"

"I'll show you how to make it, Mum, shall I?"

"Yes, darling, but not tonight. You need a bath and I'm a bit tired."

"So am I," Lettie chimed in, quick as usual to sense that Serena was upset and would probably confide in her once Nicky was settled. But he was over-excited and it took much longer to finally get him to sleep.

When she came through to the

kitchen, she found Lettie had prepared a light salad meal for them both, with a bottle of Frascati in the fridge to chill.

"Now then, love, out with it." Later with coffee on the low table between them, the lamplight giving a soft glow, Lettie turned to the young woman, her eyes full of ready sympathy. "What happened, Serena?"

"Oh Lettie — we've finished, Matthew and me! I — I couldn't pretend, couldn't sleep with him. He wanted me to, and to promise to marry him." Between the soft convulsive little sobs, the words were disjointed, but the meaning was clear. "I don't think I really love him. I don't want second best, Lettie."

Her arms clasped across her body, she rocked herself as if for comfort.

"So — we've split up! He's going up north to work, for a while anyway. He was *so* angry; called me awful names . . . " She bit her lip, remembering. "He apologized after.

I know it was just frustration, his disappointment, but — well, everything was spoiled and ugly. So we came home."

Lettie stirred her coffee, her eyes thoughtful.

"You'll miss him, love."

"I know." The tears spilled over again. "But he'd been asking me, pushing me for an answer — but I couldn't. I'd rather go without sex."

Her face flushed and Lettie murmured. "I know, pet. You're not the type to sleep with a man unless you loved him completely." She rose and refilled their coffee mugs.

"Don't worry, you're still young enough to wait until the right man comes along. And when he does . . . "

"Will I know, Lettie?" Watching the downcast head, the curtain-fall of bright hair, the young girl's soft plea made Lettie's heart ache. Poor kid, she'd had a rotten deal out of life up to now, except for her little boy.

"You'll know, pet," she answered quietly.

"I just want to be the first — the only one to the man I love," Serena answered.

"Meanwhile, you've got Nicky. You're first with him, aren't you?"

"Bless you, Lettie, you're an angel." With an obvious effort to change the subject, Serena suggested, "How about watching that film?"

But both women were only giving eye-service to the television screen; both were busy with their thoughts and trying not to show it.

* * *

Her boss came into her office as soon as arrived the next day.

"Morning, Serena, how did your weekend go?" And then he looked, really looked, at her face. "What happened — or don't you want to tell me?"

"Hello, Walter." She paused, not

knowing how to answer. Then, deciding that he would find out sooner or later, she told him, "Not a very good weekend. We split up, Matthew and me. He — he wanted to marry me, but I found I didn't really want him as a husband."

"Just as a fond friend?" Walter's voice was full of gentle understanding. "Better to find out this side of the marriage service, my dear. I'm sorry though, you deserve a little happiness now.

"Thanks, Walter." With a sigh, she turned to the morning's work. "There's a rumour of blight in the Medoc area . . . "

When she went upstairs for lunch, Lettie told her, "There was a phone call for you about eleven o'clock." Something in her voice made Serena's heart skip a beat.

"Oh — who was it?"

"She didn't say, but it was a foreign-sounding voice. All she said was she would be coming here this evening and would you please be sure to be in. A haughty piece she sounded."

Serena smiled at Lettie's disgust. "Perhaps just someone pushing a new wine. Thought she'd have a better chance after office hours. Don't worry, Lettie, I'll soon get rid of her if it is."

Later, by the time they had eaten their evening meal, Serena had almost forgotten all about the phone call. Nicky was still full of his weekend with the other children, and as she read him a bedtime story, she wondered if he was lonely; needing a brother or sister?

Lettie had already left for her weekly whist drive when the night porter announced her visitor.

"Oh damn!" She was just about to work on some lists she hadn't had time for all day. "Thanks, send her up." Glancing round to see if the lounge was tidy, she straightened her hair and went to the lift. Her first impression of the tall woman before her was of the haughty way she held

110

her dark head, the cold scrutiny of the coal-black eyes, of thin lips set in a sallow-skinned face.

"Good evening," she began courteously. "I don't believe we've met . . . "

"*I-Io sono* Lucia Ercoli — sister to Roberto and Gino."

"Gino's sister! Oh please, do come in," Serena stretched out her hand, a welcoming smile on her face. *"Molto lieto. Come sta?"*

Ignoring the outstretched hand, the Italian woman looked around the room disdainfully.

"I have come to take *suo figlio* — your son to see his *nonno and nonna* — his grandparents. My father is *malato* — ill and needs to see his grandson."

Without waiting for an invitation, she moved to the settee placing a beautiful leather bag beside her as she sat down and crossed her long thin legs. Everything about her spoke of wealth; her *haute couture* suit, the hand-made shoes exactly matching her

111

handbag, gleaming pearls round her throat and in her ear lobes.

But it struck Serena at once that the brothers had inherited the good looks in the Ercoli family for there was nothing beautiful about the Signorina Lucia. The cold contempt in her dark eyes sent a chill through Serena's veins. She could almost feel the other's dislike reaching out across the room. Then the words came back . . .

"To take Nicky? *Non posso* — I can't let you do that. He doesn't know you and he's far too young to go to Italy without me!"

"He belongs to Casa d'Ercoli with his father's family, not here, the *povero bambino*." From her attitude, it would seem that Nicky was living in a veritable slum, and Serena felt her anger rise.

"*Signorina*, for eight years the Ercoli family chose to ignore my son and me. I agree that he should get to know his grandparents, but *I* shall say where and when, not you or your brother Roberto."

Thin lips curled as the Italian woman answered, "Gino did not tell us he was married or had a child. Since his death and we found out, we think he was too ashamed of you — that you had been maybe *una puttana*!" She almost spat out the last insult.

"Prostitute!" Serena choked, almost speechless. "How dare you? I was an eighteen-year-old virgin when I married Gino! After Nicky's birth, we practically separated; he preferred to change his partners every few months. So I refused him my bed. I've slept alone ever since. Not that it is your business!"

Blind anger made her colour deepen; she could hardly speak for the lump constricting her throat. Lucia Ercoli shrugged her thin shoulders and her eyes were full of insolence and disbelief. As she rose, she towered above Serena.

"That is as maybe. We do not need to quarrel. I only came for Nico. It would be better for you if you did as I request. Please make the necessary arrangements and I will collect him on

Saturday from here."

She placed a heavily embossed visiting card on the coffee table.

"*Mai* — never! I would never trust you with my little boy. Please, *andare via*! Go away and don't ever come back."

Suddenly Serena saw red. She reached out to push this cold-faced insolent woman towards the lift.

"You will hear from me!" With this last threat, Lucia Ercoli pressed the down button and the lift gates closed, leaving Serena panting with furious indignation. She would never trust her son in the hands of that woman. Some deep instinct told her that she didn't really want him at the Casa d'Ercoli. As she read the calling card, she saw for the first time the proper address of her late husband's family home.

4

"I SHOULD have thought the last thing she'd want is to have Nicky over there. Surely she'd rather he didn't share in the family fortune? More for Roberto and Lucia, I reckon, if the old couple never got to know him." Lettie paused and then grimaced. "Or am I just being nasty?"

She knew her old dislike and distrust of Serena's dead husband could well be colouring her doubts about his family. But from Serena's description, the Signorina Lucia Ercoli sounded every bit as devious as Gino had been.

"She made my blood run cold. Ugh! Her eyes were so hard, so full of hatred. But what have I ever done to her?"

Lettie poured out the hot drinks she'd just made and shook her head.

"Don't worry, pet. I'll see her off if

115

she does turn up on Saturday, never fear."

"All the same, I do think Nicky should see his grandparents. He'll have time off from school for Easter soon; maybe I should take him then?" Serena fingered once more the embossed card Lucia had left. "The Casa d'Ercoli seems to be on the Lake Garda, somewhere near Bardolino."

"Isn't that one of your wine places?" Over the years, Lettie had picked up quite a good bit about the wine trade.

"That's right. I think it's a lovely spot. But I wouldn't want to travel until all the Easter celebrations are over." Thoughtfully, Serena sipped the hot drink. "What do you think, Lettie? Do you think I'd be all right taking him over by myself?"

"Well, do you want me to go with you?" Lettie asked.

"No, I don't think so. Walter might need a hand downstairs — part-time anyway. Just in the front shop; would you do that? I don't want to leave

116

him in the lurch, though I'm due some time off."

Rinsing the mugs at the sink, Lettie answered thoughtfully, "Think it out well first, love."

★ ★ ★

The next morning Walter was delighted with the suggestion.

"Do you good, my dear. And the lad; he should know he has two sets of grandparents like other little boys. Take all the time you need."

"But how will you manage?"

Walter's bushy eyebrows rose, his brown eyes twinkling.

"Oh, I think we'd just about get by," he teased.

"You know what I mean," Serena laughed.

"M'm. I could borrow a chap from one of the branches, say for three days a week?"

"And Lettie says she'll help out in the front for a few days each week."

Walter beamed. "Good. I might persuade her to feed me lunch upstairs on the other days."

Again Serena smiled, knowing how much he liked her friend's cooking.

"Look, my dear, take your time. Sort out all the arrangements thoroughly, carefully, beforehand. Let me know if I can help. Got your passport?"

"Yes," she nodded, "but I'll need to get one for Nicky. Oh, Walter, I wonder what he'll say?"

"He'll love it." Walter smiled knowingly. "His first time in a plane?" Serena nodded, a faint frown on her brow.

"First time abroad too. Do you think he's too young?"

"Of course not! He won't be thrilled by the old churches and so on, but as for the rest . . . yes, he'll love it."

On Saturday, Serena took Nicky for his weekly swimming lesson. Along with several other young mothers and their offspring, she had a great time splashing about, watching with pride as her little son swam the width of the pool with only his bright plastic armbands for support.

"See, Mum, I told you I could swim. Next week I'm not having these on." His look of disgust as she pulled off the safety armbands all too clear.

He's growing up fast, she mused, as she towelled his dark hair. He'd always been rather precocious and articulate — perhaps from being with adults so much. But she had always been pleased that he showed signs of having a deeper, more serious side to his character than his father.

As they sat in the balcony café overlooking the pool, she began to talk about the idea of their going to Italy.

"Your *nonno* and *nonna* want to see you, so I thought we'd go to Italy, you and I, and see where your papa was born. What do you think?" Sipping her coffee, she watched his face closely from beneath her lashes, wondering if the mention of his father would upset him. But it didn't seem to, and he was thrilled by the thought of going to Italy.

"Shall we fly, mum?"

"Of course! Won't that be great?" Nicky pushed his beaker around, a pensive look on his face. He was thinking seriously about something she could tell.

"I want to go to Venice," he announced firmly. "Y'know, Mum, that place that's all water, no streets, no roads." There was a hint of disbelief in his voice, but he went on, "Can we, please? I do want to go to Venice. Then we could see *nonno* and *nonna* afterwards, couldn't we?" Two large dark eyes looked up beseechingly and she couldn't refuse him.

"What a good idea of yours, pet!" His chest swelled several inches at that. "Of course we can; we'll go there first. It's quite near really to their place. We'll get a map and I'll show you."

His voice was full of excitement as he said goodbye to his pals, telling them eagerly, "I'm going to Italy — that's abroad — in a plane." And their obvious envy pleased him no end!

On the way home, he was even more delighted to have his passport photo taken in an automatic booth. It took three times before an unblurred one was finally taken.

★ ★ ★

"What a nasty piece of work that one is!" The disgust on Lettie's homely face was almost comical. "She was so mad when I told her you were both out. And that there was no way you'd be letting her take Nicky back to Italy with her."

"Oh dear, I seem to have let you in for an awkward time." Serena's face showed her dismay, but actually Lettie had quite enjoyed the confrontation with the haughty Lucia Ercoli.

"She's not bothered about Nicky really. She didn't ask to see him the other night, did she?" Not as Roberto had, Serena recalled to herself. "I

121

reckon she's just a sour old maid, but I wouldn't trust her an inch! You should have heard her; not that I understood much of what she said," Lettie went on, "but the look on her face was bad enough."

"I'm sorry you had to face her, Lettie."

"Don't worry, love, I gave her plenty back, cool, calm and to the point. I don't think she'll be back again."

"Do you think I should let them know I'm coming?" Serena asked.

In the kitchen, lunch was nearly ready, and they had been discussing Lucia Ercoli's visit. The housekeeper stirred the contents of a saucepan before she answered, "Wait until you've got all your arrangements fixed, and then drop them a line to say you're bringing Nicky to see his grandparents. Then take things as they come. It's no good getting all worked up before then, pet," Lettie finished wisely.

★ ★ ★

The following Monday, Serena took an early lunch and hurried out into the pale sunshine, suddenly feeling more excited about the trip. The girl in Thomas Cook's was most helpful.

"I want to go to Venice for two nights, and then travel on to Lake Garda. I'll have my young son with me; he needs a passport." Serena opened her bag to get out Nicky's small photo. The three of them had spent a long time on Sunday poring over a map of Italy; looking at pictures of Venice and Lake Garda. Nicky had already planned what he wanted to take in his duffel bag.

Now, with brochures and timetables in front of her, the girl said, "I suggest you fly from Gatwick to the Marco Polo airport; it's just on the mainland, about two hours' flight."

"And then?" Serena queried.

"Let me see — you take a motor bus across the lagoon to Jetty 1 of the vaporetto line and on to your hotel. We'll book that for you; arrange about your luggage, everything."

"And after the two nights, I'll need a hire car to Lake Garda. Can that be arranged too?" Serena enquired.

"Certainly, Mrs Ercoli, we'll supply route maps, currency, travellers' cheques, all you need. Leave it all to us." The girl was pleasantly efficient and Serena left the office feeling she could do just that. All she needed to do was sign the cheque!

Whether it was the early spring sunshine, or the relief she felt at having got things underway, she wasn't sure, but her heart suddenly felt lighter. And in a fit of extravagance she decided to buy herself some new clothes. Cotton frocks with matching little jackets, cool slinky cocktail dresses, smart tops with full skirts to tone. And as a last defiant gesture, a couple of smart bikinis.

And as she tried these on, she was pleased to see that the lines of her figure were still firm and young looking.

It was as she was waiting for a delighted salesgirl to wrap her purchases, she saw it . . . a lovely crepe silk dress in black. The price on the swing ticket made her wince. On the hanger, nothing showed of the wonderful lines, the cunning fit that was displayed when she tried it on. She had heard of the smart Italian clothes worn over there and black, as well as being for mourning, suited her blonde colouring so well, she told herself.

"Oh, that's for you!" For once the salesgirl forgot the commission and really meant it! Serena turned, trying to see first the side view and then the rear, her voice uncertain but with longing in her heart.

"But it's so expensive!" The protest was but a token one however.

"Worth every penny. It was just made for you," the girl enthused. And Serena was lost.

"I'll take it." Downstairs in the children's department, she bought several cute T-shirts for Nicky, shorts too. She knew they'd have to shop together for sandals and trainers. He would also want to choose a couple of new anoraks for himself, but at the last moment, she added two pairs of swim trunks for him, smiling at their smallness. Loaded down with parcels, she took a taxi back to work, sent a lad upstairs with her purchases and then settled down to making up for lost time.

There was so much to do before they went. She had to see Nicky's headmistress in case they stayed longer than the school holidays.

"Don't worry, Mrs Ercoli, your son's a bright little chap; he'll soon make up for any missed lessons." Her eyes softened for a moment, and then she added softly, "I was very sorry to hear of your husband's death, but I believe Nicky's got over it, and I hope the break will do you both good. I really envy you." The older woman's face was tired; she looked as if she needed a holiday herself.

A keen young man from one of the outer London branches came in for a few days and Serena was pleased to see how quickly he settled in.

"I want you to take things a bit easier while we're away, Lettie. Take some time off, won't you?"

"Don't worry, pet, I've got my own plans." But she didn't say what they were. "By the way, I'll drive you to the airport and see you off."

★ ★ ★

It was hard to get Nicky down to sleep the night before their departure. Lettie had been giving him last-minute instructions.

"Don't forget, love, to stay close to your mother. Watch over the luggage while she's busy with passports and so on, won't you? And don't get talking to strangers." Her voice was thick, her eyes glistened with the tears she was trying to hold back.

With gentle understanding, Serena hugged her close.

"Don't worry, Lettie, we'll take care of each other, won't we Nicky?"

"I won't have to hold your hand, will I?" At the disgust on his face, she hugged him too.

"Of course not. But I really do want you to stay close or else *I* might get lost!" All three of them smiled at that, but the eyes of both women were moist. They were very close, and would miss each other.

Nicky was so excited when they finally reached the airport Serena thought he'd make himself ill. He wanted to see everything at once.

"How about helping me to push this trolley?" she coaxed.

"I can do it myself," he insisted, but she made sure her hand guided it through the bustling crowds.

Once in the noisy lounge, he glued his nose to the huge windows overlooking the tarmac, pointing out all the different planes, pausing to identify the directions coming over the tannoy. At last their plane was announced and as Serena clutched his hand she felt it tremble in hers.

"I'm always a bit scared at first," she told him. "Still with you beside me I think I'll be all right." Just then the queue moved forward, pushing Nicky away from her. A tall, thin man in front of her blocked her view and just for a moment she felt a tremor of fear.

"Mum, you'll get lost, come here." Following his sturdy little figure, she entered the plane to be greeted by a dark-eyed stewardess, and she felt a surge of pride at Nicky's courteous reply in Italian.

He was given a window seat, but his gaze was everywhere; watching wide-eyed as the stewardess went through the customary procedures regarding emergencies, tightening his seat belt, checking that his mother had fastened hers too.

A few knuckle-clenching moments later and the plane left the runway to soar heavenwards like a huge bird. Thrilled, Nicky pointed out, "Look at the clouds, Mum — just like the cottonwool balls in the bathroom. I can't see the houses and fields now."

"We'll be over the English Channel soon."

"And then over France." Nicky had learned his lesson well from the maps. He was utterly fascinated by the meal they were served, so taken up by the little tray, the plastic cutlery and tiny packets of salt and pepper, that he almost forgot to eat. Childlike he poked about, sorting out what he liked, discarding the rest.

"I'd like coffee, please," he told the stewardess firmly. Serena was about to point out that he wasn't keen on coffee normally, and then held her tongue, realizing he wanted to try out his other packets! Later, however, she asked for a Coke and received a grateful grin.

"I need the loo, Mum."

"That's it over there; you'll have to join the queue. Can you manage?"

"Of course!" All the same, she was pleased when an elderly lady in the queue showed him how the cabin door worked. Soon he was back, bursting to tell her all about the wonders of toilets on a plane!

Wriggling in his seat, he chatted about their stay in Venice and then seeing *Nonno* and *Nonna* Ercoli when they got to Bardolino.

"Shush, darling," she urged. Was his chatter disturbing the passenger taking the third seat, she wondered? For the first time she half turned, and to her confusion, found that the man seated there was watching them intently and had obviously been listening to all Nicky's prattle. She recognized the man whose tall figure had hidden her son's for that scary brief moment.

Feeling her colour rise, she turned back quickly and diverted Nicky's attention by opening his latest comic. To her relief, a few minutes later, his head began to nod and he fell asleep leaning against her shoulder. Somehow she wasn't too keen on half the plane knowing all about their journey!

"Wake up, darling, and fasten your seat belt. We're here." Like most children, Nicky was fully alert in seconds, craning his neck to catch his first glimpse of Italy as the steps were wheeled to the exit. Helping his mother collect their hand luggage, he solemnly bade the stewardess a very grown-up *"Addio, grazie"* and scampered down the steps.

"It's warm here, isn't it, Mum?" Indeed the air was degrees warmer than that in London and she lifted her face to the sun with a happy sigh. Once through the customs, they were soon aboard one of the motoscafi taking them across the lagoon to Venice proper.

"It's like the sea." Nicky leaned over the railing fascinated by the lapping waves. The sun shining on the water seemed to be scattering silver coins, and to his delight, the passing of all the different kinds of water craft made theirs rock from side to side.

"Be careful, pet. Don't lean over too much."

Serena could see that she'd have to

watch him carefully once they reached Venice. Yet she hated to nag him or curb his exuberance.

At the first landing stage, he helped her check that their bags were aboard, then he wanted to see everything at once. The medley of traffic on the Grand Canal enchanted him, and he turned from side to side, pointing it out excitedly.

"Look, Mum, it's a gondola — a real one! He's standing up to row it." Then in a tone of disgust, "The buildings are all old and broken down. And look, the water's going into that one. Won't the people in there drown?"

"They live upstairs, pet — see, there's a flight of steps up the side there."

"Will there be water in our hotel?" She could see he wasn't keen on the idea of water in the buildings.

"No, I'm sure there won't."

Once more she clutched the back of his anorak, holding him tightly while he leaned over to watch the next landing stage come closer. As she looked round, deep pleasure filled her heart. How she loved Venice the Beautiful — the faded pink facades, the tiny white bridges, the narrow little backwaters.

"È bella, non è vero, la Venezia?" Nicky turned, dark eyes alight with wonder and replied,

"Si, sir. È bellissima." Her boy was half Italian, she mused and right then that half was all too evident! In this land of dark-eyed, black-haired Latins, he merged as she never would.

The Hotel Suisse was quite near to the Piazza San Marco, and their luggage was being unloaded at the rear as they collected their key from the small reception desk.

"Signora Ercoli and *suo figlio — piccolo ragazzo — viso d'angelo . . . "*

The fuss they made of Nicky soon had him pink-faced with embarrassment.

"You'd think I was a baby!" he muttered as the old-fashioned wrought-iron lift clanked its way up to the second floor.

"You'll get used to it, pet," she told

him gently. "You see all Italians adore small children. I'm sure they think you live here. Don't let it bother you."

But the look of scorn on his face right then was very English! They had a twin-bedded room with its own small bathroom. Unfortunately there was no view to speak of, but 'the funny taps' over the bath kept Nicky amused as she unpacked.

"Let's go out, Mum, shall we?" He was eager to explore, but once outside the hotel entrance, he asked, "Shall we get lost?" Patiently Serena explained how easy it was to follow the signs on each corner of the buildings.

"We follow the arrow pointing to San Marco, it's easy." They made a beautiful pair — Serena so cool and fair, and her small son so dark-eyed and sturdy. More than one pair of Latin eyes followed their progress. She longed to browse round the elegant shops, but Nicky wanted to clamber up the steps and over the bridges. St Mark's Square had *him* spellbound for its flocks of fat pigeons, not the arcades of shops or the wonderful buildings.

She bought him a packet of bird seed and sat in the fading sunshine watching his delight as the ever-greedy birds flocked around his feet. Tomorrow she would take him into the Basilica of St Mark's with a quick look round the Doge's Palace, and perhaps if he wasn't too bored, up the tall bell tower. Just then up above, the figures of the Moors struck the hour and after that she had the greatest trouble getting him away. He wanted to wait until they did it again.

"We must get back, Nicky, and change for dinner," she urged.

"Dinner? Will it be awful?" And his grimace said, "as bad as school dinners?"

"Of course not. You know you like spaghetti and all the pastas. Here it'll be food alla Venezia, but I'll ask for something you'll like, don't worry, darling." She gave him a fond smile. "It'll be long past your bedtime, but tonight you're going to escort your mother in to dinner at a nice hotel," and at that he gave a deep sigh of pleasure.

Seated later at their little table for two, she in a smart, cool dress, Nicky in clean cotton pants and matching shirt, they made a charming sight. Several guests' eyes had followed their progress to the table. To Serena's amusement, the besotted waiters overwhelmed them with attention, making a fuss of Nicky, ensuring that he got exactly what he wanted and at once! And as he chatted to them happily in very good Italian, she could see he was beginning to like this adulation.

What to do at night for this short stay was the problem. She couldn't go out, even nearby, and leave him, could she? They found the low-voltage lighting in the room was too dim to read by comfortably. The television was highly comical with a tough John Wayne talking in soft Italian. But tired out by the long day, he was soon asleep, leaving Serena lying on her bed, staring wide-eyed up at the carved ceiling, wondering what her reception at the Casa d'Ercoli would be like. The thought of clashing again with Lucia Ercoli sent a tremor of dread through her. As for Roberto, that cold, arrogant man, she wouldn't trust him either . . .

Then suddenly she remembered the tenderness on his face as he had looked at Nicky, asleep in his little bed. Did either of them want him at the Casa d'Ercoli? Somehow she doubted it, and wished the visit was over.

The noise of the church bells woke her early the next morning — that and the clatter of the long flat boat beneath their window collecting rubbish!

"Let me see, Mum," and before she could stop him, Nicky was leaning right out of the window, vastly amused at having their overflowing bins emptied by boat! Leaving him calling out to the men below, Serena took a quick shower and put on a chic cotton dress with a short matching jacket, well aware that bare feminine arms were frowned upon in Italian churches.

Nicky loved his hot roll and cherry jam and was soon given more by his doting waiter. The dining-room was half empty, but Serena noticed one or two from their plane had also booked in there.

As the morning wore on, she was thankful for her comfortable sandals. As for Nicky he didn't seem to feel the heat at all. As she expected, he quickly got bored with sightseeing, except that is for the dungeons near the Bridge of Sighs and the view from the top of the Bell Tower.

The square was crowded by then, with package-tour guides trying to keep their straying flocks together, students squatting on the steps; the tongues of every nationality creating a constant babel all around. Serena was content to sit in the sun drinking her espresso coffee, listening to the orchestra playing behind her.

"I want to go somewhere else, Mum." Nicky was bored, too young to be happy to sit and see and be seen.

"OK, wipe your mouth, pet." He had a moustache of white froth from his milk shake.

The little back streets were cooler, but still as crowded, and she had difficulty in keeping him in sight. Up and over the bridges, on fast feet to the next canal bank; leaning over, craning to see everything beyond the surging crowds.

For a moment, she lost sight of him and again she knew that pang of fear as it clutched her breast.

Calling, "Nicky — wait," she struggled anxiously past the group blocking her way, but she couldn't see him and her throat tightened with fear, her legs turning to jelly. Then she heard a sudden splash, followed by cries of alarm, raised voices . . .

Panic-stricken now, she pushed desperately, trying to see . . . to find her son. On both sides, she heard snatches of alarm.

"*Povero bambino*. In the canal. He's fallen in . . . "

She was to have nightmares afterwards for ages, but right then her heart froze with fear, her throat gripped by the shock.

"Nicky! Oh God, he's in the water." With superhuman strength she finally cleared herself a path through the onlookers. And then she saw him — calmly swimming awkwardly to the bank. "Oh Nicky . . . "

Throwing herself on her knees to the ground, she stretched out, struggling to pull him out of the dank water, gripping him close, shaking with shock and relief.

"See, Mum, I told you I could swim."

For one blazing moment, she felt like lashing out at him.

"I've told you — not to lean too far over — to be careful not to fall in," she gasped, her throat still choked by that awful fear.

"I didn't fall in." He stood there dripping, his dark hair plastered round his wet face, his little chest heaving. "Somebody pushed me!"

Still half-sobbing, half-angry, Serena began to squeeze the filthy water from his hair, his T-shirt and shorts. Thank heavens it was so warm she thought; he'd be almost dry by the time they reached the hotel.

"Come along, let's hurry and get you changed." Would he be ill from the effects of the canal water? He'd had all his jabs as a baby, but could he be sick or poisoned? As they hurried along, the frantic thoughts ran round her mind.

A chambermaid, taking clean linen to their room, left her trolley, her hands spread wide in horror.

"Signora Ercoli, *cosa c'e*? What is the matter with *povero bambino*?" After a few words of explanation, she offered to take his clothes to the laundry and return them later that evening. Serena gave Nicky a

142

good scrub down under the shower ignoring his protests. She did leave him to dry himself and get into clean clothes while she sat slumped in a chair, reliving that heart-stopping moment of terror. She was disgusted at herself for going to pieces, and she was still trembling. Nicky, however, thought the whole incident a giggle, an adventure!

"But I told you not to go too close," she repeated wearily.

"But someone pushed me, like I told you, Mum."

"I don't want to hear excuses, a lie." Her anger covered the fright still pounding away inside her.

"It's not a lie!" She looked at her son's red face; could she believe him? He wasn't given to lying, was he? "Somebody behind me pushed me. I felt — a big hand, here, in my back and I fell in. I couldn't help it, Mum, honestly. *Vero, vero*," he repeated hotly, realizing then what it had done to his mother.

Putting his arm across her shoulder, he said softly, "I can swim, Mum. I was a bit frightened when I went under the water. It was all greeny dark. Then I remembered I can swim. I'm sorry, Mum."

Not wanting to worry him, she pulled herself together and hugged him close.

"Let's go and get some lunch, shall we, pet?"

"Oh good, I'm starved."

"Well, if you will go swimming with your clothes on." Her smile was an effort, but right then she didn't want him to see how upset she was. Had someone deliberately pushed her son into the canal? Of course not, the whole idea was ridiculous! You often get nudged when in a crowd.

Nicky wanted to eat as they walked along, like the other tourists, so she settled for an Italian 'toast' — a slice of ham and one of cheese between two rounds of bread until all melted together. He was delighted with the

144

special little paper squares used to eat this way.

"How about going to see them blowing glass, Nicky — making all these little glass figures?" she suggested when they'd finished eating.

"Can we? Yes, let's."

Wide-eyed, he watched enthralled as the red-tipped rods of glass were twirled and twisted into intricate shapes. She had to restrain him from buying too many of the tiny animal figurines.

"I'll take *Nonno* and *Nonna* one. And one for Lettie." The list grew. But she couldn't refuse him, and watched fondly as the girl carefully wrapped his purchases for him.

In and out of the narrow alleyways; sitting in quiet piazzas licking cones of colourful gelato, and always returning to meander along the banks of the Grand Canal, so different from the Thames back home.

"Look Mum, at that big black boat. What is it?"

For once, Serena was loath to answer

him. "It's a funeral boat. It takes the coffins to a special little island cemetery. They say it's very beautiful." She waited, hoping he wasn't going to ask more about it.

"Well, that's better than chucking them into the water, isn't it?" Funny how a child's mind works, she mused.

"Can we go on one of those boats for a ride, Mum, please? One of those with a music man in." So they joined the other tourists in a small flotilla of boats accompanied by an accordion player, in and out of the backwaters, almost beneath the debris being tipped out occasionally from the windows high above.

Watching Nicky as he trailed his fingers over the side of the boat, she felt that he'd really enjoyed his trip to Venice, although he was far too young to appreciate its historical beauty.

After dinner that night, he was soon fast asleep and the friendly young maid persuaded Serena to leave him in her care.

"I will come in to see him many times, Signora Ercoli, never fear."

"Well, I'll just go down to the lounge for a little while. *Grazie.*"

But she felt rather conspicuous sitting drinking her carafe of wine alone, and as they had an early start in the morning, she decided to go up to her room.

"He has been — er — restless, *signora*." The young girl struggled for the words. "But I soothed him well. Now he sleeps."

"*Grazie.* You are very *gentile, grazie.*" Serena slipped a note into the girl's willing hand, and then hurried in to see if Nicky was still asleep. As she dropped a soft kiss on his cheek, he stirred sleepily.

"I saw the maid, Mum. Then that man . . . "

"Man? What man, darling?" But he was asleep again. He must have been dreaming about a man, she told herself.

However, when she started to pack

the next morning, she found that someone *had* been in their room — the drawers had been ransacked, everything disturbed. Dismayed, her brows creased with worry. Should she tell the manager and let him get the police? But that would delay their departure. It had probably been an opportunist thief, taking advantage of the unlocked door, she thought to herself worriedly. Nothing seemed to be missing — perhaps the maid had disturbed him? Had Nicky really seen a man last night?

For a moment, she wished she had someone with her, someone she could depend on and trust. Then Nicky called from the bathroom and she pulled herself together. She was not a child; she could take care of herself and her son.

All the same, down in the dining-room she could hardly swallow her croissant and drank an extra cup of coffee instead. On the boat back to landing stage one, she found herself nervously glancing over her shoulder. She couldn't shake off the feeling that someone was watching them.

Once across the lagoon, she contacted the car-hire firm's depot.

"The tank is full, Signora Ercoli. Here are the papers and the map you requested."

"I don't know how long I shall need the car," she began, only to be assured that she could keep it as long as required. Her booking agent had made all the necessary arrangements.

"It is a good car, *si*." The efficient girl smiled broadly and patted the sturdy little Fiat.

"I hope so." Serena hated driving a strange car, or driving on the right, but she knew she'd soon get used to both again.

Spreading out the map, she saw that the road to Bardolino was a good one, clearly marked, and that she could skirt Verona by taking a slightly longer route. The scenery was beautiful and she wished she didn't have to concentrate

149

so hard on her driving. The lush green fields with the hills rising in the distance looked so inviting . . .

Suddenly a terrible noise in the engine brought her back with a jerk.

"What's the matter, Mum?" Nicky was alarmed, and just for then so was she. Pulling into the side of the road with a juddering stop she applied the brakes, her hand shaking.

Nicky tugged at her arm. "What shall we do?" he asked anxiously.

"Don't worry, pet. Someone will be along who'll help us." They both got out of the car, glancing hopefully at the passing traffic. But in spite of her uplifted hand, it ignored her. Until a ramshackle old lorry pulled up with a screech and a red-faced driver leaned out.

"*Cosa c'e?*" he asked.

"My car's broken down. Can you send someone to tow it?"

With a shrug of fat shoulders, he shook his head, turned to his equally plump mate in the seat beside him.

With much gesticulation and a flood of rapid Italian, he leaned out once more, thick eyebrows raised.

Serena tried again in Italian.

"Ho un guasto alla macchina. Pùo mandare qualcuno a rimorchiarla?"

"Si, si." With a great deal of puffing and blowing, he got down and helped them into the cabin, explaining that he would take them to a nearby *villaggio* where there was a good mechanic and a café. Diving into the back, the driver's mate produced a thick, tattered rope and hitched the car to the rear bumper, got inside, and they set off.

"This is good, isn't it, Mum?" Beside her on the lumpy seat, Nicky wriggled excitedly. "You can see much better from up here."

But she was far too worried to enjoy the adventure. Perhaps she would need to contact the hire firm if this car was going to give her trouble? The sleepy little village was very quiet, and their strange convoy made what locals that were around turn to stare.

The garage proprietor took pity on her, leaving his other work to look at the Fiat at once. For several minutes, he poked and prodded under the bonnet; grunted and then sighed. Then lugubriously he announced that someone had sheared through a vital part!

"*Cristo mio!* You could have been killed." He held up a small metal part, pointing out to their lorry driver just what had happened. With much head shaking and gesticulating, they agreed that the damage had been done deliberately.

"But how? Why? I can't understand it!" Exasperated, the tears were burning behind Serena's eyelids, and suddenly she was terribly worried. On top of the thought of last evening's intruder, this was too much.

"I will mend for you, *signora*, never fear. You and the little one go and find some coffee, or even something a little stronger, si," he added with a cheerful grin. Biting her bottom lip, she locked the car doors and the boot, thanked the lorry driver, who refused a tip and told the mechanic they would be in the café bar opposite.

"Somebody tried to wreck the car, didn't they, Mum?" For once she wished Nicky's Italian wasn't so good. To allay his fears, she tried to make light of it.

"You know what garages are like, pet . . . " she laughed. "Want a fruit juice, a Coke, or a milk shake?"

The little café was poorly furnished, though spotlessly clean. Two wrinkle-faced locals sat reading their papers at one table, and a mother with a fractious baby tried to drink her espresso at another. As she ordered their drinks, she was surprised to find that the proprietor already knew of their predicament. Bad news had good legs around there it seemed!

It was two hours later before the car was ready and she had to use her currency to pay the helpful mechanic; he didn't trust travellers' cheques. As she took the road again, the fear niggled away inside her. Were all their mishaps just coincidences, or was someone doing these things deliberately? And if so — who . . . ?

5

THE sun was higher in the sky, the temperature rising all the time, and both Serena and Nicky were hot and sticky and thirsty. In the distance, the hills, thick with vegetation, looked dark and cool.

"I think we'll stop for something to eat and drink, shall we, love? She pushed the hair from her damp forehead, noticing that Nicky looked tired and flushed too. "Look out for a decent-looking hotel; then we can get a wash and tidy-up first."

The reflection from the white buildings, the glare from the wide road was so bright after the tree-shaded countryside. In a mellow old square, they found a small hotel with a pleasant bar café in its shady annexe.

"Wash your hands and face, love. I won't be a moment." They both felt better for that, and along with tall frosted glass of *limonata* Serena ordered ham and mushroom omelettes followed by a *cassata* for Nicky and a *macedonia di frutta* — a fruit salad — for herself. They both felt repleted and refreshed, ready to face the end of the journey.

Bardolino was a beautiful place, and she fell under the spell of its charm as soon as they came into the lively town square. Tall Renaissance houses with shuttered windows and black fretted doors; shops full of smart clothes and cleverly designed household goods urged her to stop, but she resisted the temptation and decided instead to ask the way to the Casa d'Ercoli.

She pulled up alongside a delivery van and in a few moments the voluble driver had directed her to their destination. Apparently, the villa was midway between Bardolino and Garda, about three miles further on. Driving slowly, reluctantly, she noticed other large houses set back in green lush gardens, well secluded by blossoming trees and vines.

"Look, Mum, that's it! There's our name — there." Excitedly Nicky leaned out of the car window, pointing to the wrought-iron gates standing open between two tall columns bearing the name Casa d'Ercoli in the coat of arms — a wreath of vine leaves framing a bunch of grapes.

Her heart beating faster, she turned the little car into the broad, tree-lined drive. It turned and twisted for a time until one final bend gave a view of the house.

"Oh, Mum, isn't it grand?" Nicky whispered on a slow breath. And grand it was! Like so many Italian mansions, its front windows were shuttered against the heat of the sun. Three floors high, it glistened white except for the huge dark oak door in the centre; with tubs and urns of red geraniums spilling out in abundance. Where the drive split into a semi-circle, a white marble figure held aloft a scrolled jar from which a cool fountain splashed, sparkling in the bright sunlight.

Serena could just see outlines of other buildings at the side and rear; a glimpse of the dappled blue of the Lake Garda.

"Come on, Mum, let's go in." Impatiently Nicky jumped down and tugged at her arm. She took a deep breath, straightened her dress, smoothed her hair and with slim shoulders squared, she walked across to the heavy door. It wasn't locked and it opened to a square courtyard, cool and shaded with glorious flowers, splashing fountains everywhere. So beautiful and peaceful, it soothed her clamouring nerves, the rapid pulse in her throat. "Wow!" Obviously Nicky loved it too.

On the right, she pulled on a black iron door-bell and waited, her face calm and controlled, but inside her heart was still thudding rapidly.

After what seemed like an age, the heavy door was opened by an elderly grey-haired man. By his short black jacket and careful demeanour, he was evidently some sort of servant.

"Buon giorno. Io sono Signora Ercoli . . . " she began. The old man's face lit up, but it was Nicky he was looking at, his faded eyes moist with emotion.

"Si, entri, prego." With another glance at Nicky's face, he turned and they followed him into a wide hall. Serena's first impression was of sheer splendour — of furniture that was richly elegant, with curtains and rugs that were sumptuously opulent.

She followed the old man's stooped back, catching swift glimpses of rich rooms, high moulded ceilings, beautifully tiled floors, priceless antiques. As they passed one smaller room, a young girl rose from a deep settee, a glossy magazine in her hand.

"This is Signora Ercoli and her son, *signorina*."

"Thank you, Enzo." The warmth of her reply to the old man disappeared as she turned to look at Serena. Disgust, cold disdain, passed over her olive-skinned face and, as she glanced down at Nicky, that changed to positive resentment.

"Come with me. I will take you to the old ones."

For a moment, Serena's anger rose and she almost turned to go back to the car. Who was this girl; she was only about twenty? How dare she look at them like that! Nicky tugged at her dress nervously.

"She doesn't like us, does she, Mum?"

"Hush darling. Come along."

The click of the high heels, tapping out the girl's animosity, echoed across the tiled floor as she took them out into a wide conservatory. Its doors were opened to the view of green, well-tended gardens spreading down in sloping steps to the edge of the lake. Comfortable white cane furniture, low tables and stools filled this pleasant sitting-out area. On one *chaise-longue* was a man of about sixty-five. Once he

160

must have looked exactly like his two good-looking sons, and even now, in spite of his illness, he was still quite handsome. His black hair was streaked with silver, but his dark eyes were as keen as ever, his face proud and haughty looking.

At the sight of his visitors, he made to rise, but the tiny woman at his side put out a hand to restrain him. She put aside the piece of crochet in her lap and rose gracefully to her feet. She too had silver hair, but her face was unlined, her figure trim. And her eyes were wide as she gazed across at her grandson.

Serena walked up to her slowly and held out her hand, but the Signora Ercoli reached up and kissed her on both cheeks before she turned eagerly to Nicky.

"Ciao, piccolo mio. Come sta?" She reached out a tentative hand to the boy and Serena could see that it was trembling. To her delight, Nicky took it in his and like a true Latin, bent and

placed a gentle kiss on the back of his grandmother's hand.

"*Ciao*, Nonna." With a soft cry of pleasure, his grandmother drew him close, kissed his cheek and held him tight, her eyes filling with tears as she murmured softly,

"So like my Gino — a little boy again." Quietly Nicky stood in her embrace, not moving until she led him to his grandfather's long chair.

"*Ciao*, Nonno." This time Nicky bowed his head briefly before shaking his grandfather's hand. At that, the man's lips trembled a little and, as if by instinct, Nicky threw himself into the man's waiting arms. "Nonno, *mio* Nonno."

Serena felt the tears sting behind her eyelids. Now it seemed all worthwhile, the worry, the journey, the incipient fears, all were forgotten as she watched the happiness that seeing her son had brought to these grandparents.

"We must talk together, *nuora cara*, we have so much to learn of each other, about Gino . . . " The old man paused and his wife put in,

"You must take tea, rest first. I know you English like your afternoon tea." She turned to look for the young girl, but she had disappeared. "But, Maria . . . ?"

As if on cue, old Enzo came in carrying a heavy silver tray set with fine china. Without thinking, Serena hurried across and took the loaded tray from his old hands.

"Let me . . . "

"*Grazie, signora,*" and, as he moved to pull out a small table, there was an unfathomable look in his old eyes. "I have put Signora Ercoli in the Rose Room, and the young master next door to be close to his mother."

"Thank you, Enzo. But he is not a *bambino* needing his mother all the time. He has to learn now what it means to be of the House of Ercoli." There was a touch of haughty arrogance in Signor Ercoli's voice. Nicky looked at his mother, not sure what this could mean for him.

"He is only seven years old, Nonno; it is his first time here in Italy. I prefer him near to me for a while." Her voice was adamant. She intended to start as she meant to go on, beginning with her parents-in-law!

She was remembering she had still to face her sister and brother-in-law. And she wasn't looking forward to meeting either again! Perhaps her stand had its effect for the old man began chatting quietly to Nicky, asking him about his school, his hobbies and friends. And gradually Nicky lost all reticence and the two, so alike in features, heads close together, began getting to know each other.

"But where are the grapes to make the wine?" Nicky asked. "I thought there'd be rows and rows of them here."

"Not here, *piccino*. See, up there — those dark hills? It is up there we grow the grapes that make our wines."

"Shall I see them, Nonno?"

"Of course, Nico. Soon we all move up there for the summer. It is cooler and later everyone works in the vineyard."

"Do we sleep in huts?"

The old man chuckled. "*Cabina*? No, no, we have a good old *casa* up there, very — " he paused, seeking the right word — "comfortable for all of us." The boy's eyes gleamed and Serena couldn't help thinking that he was becoming more Italianate every minute.

"I think we'll take a rest now, pet, and I'll unpack."

"Ask Maria to help you, *cara*," suggested her mother-in-law. Was Maria one of the staff? As if reading Serena's mind, the older woman went on, "Maria Donati is a dear girl, daughter of old friends."

At that, her husband gave a slight cough, leaving Serena wondering why? On the floor above, the Rose Room was exquisitely beautiful with walls covered in cream silk with large pink cabbage roses woven in it. The curtains and covers were to match. She went across to the long window. There was a small balcony overlooking the gardens and the view of the lake.

"I've got a little balcony too, Mum. It's super here, isn't it? But I'd like to go up there where the grapes grow, wouldn't you?"

"We'll see, pet. Now have a little rest on your bed, m'm?" She unpacked his things first, moving quietly and quickly, and he was asleep by the time his clothes were all tucked away.

* * *

The sun had lowered and her room was cooler when she woke, startled for a second, wondering where she was. She showered and put on a plain, well-cut dress and a blue necklace that matched the blue stones in the slim bracelet Gino had given her on her eighteenth birthday. And as she clasped it round her wrist, she thought of how long ago that seemed now.

Nicky dressed in a smart shirt with a toning bow tie, declared that he was starving. Together they went downstairs to find her relatives gathered in the lounge next to the dining-room.

"You rested well, Serena?" There was a gentle warmth in Nonna's question as she greeted them. Signor Ercoli sat on the settee, a rug over his knees, pleasure lighting his face.

"Come here, little one." With a coaxing smile on his face, he patted a place beside him for Nicky.

"So you came then!" Serena swivelled round, the delight in the homely scene shattered by the harsh voice.

"Hello, Lucia. Yes, I came, as I promised, to bring my son to meet his grandparents." Her reply was cool, and she made no attempt to kiss Lucia's cheek or offer her hand.

With a shrug of her bony shoulders, the older woman replied, "They are easy to deceive, the older ones. They have no other grandchildren. But one day they will ask themselves *why* Gino kept his marriage to you — the birth of a child — from his family. Why you never came to see them before now? And that perhaps it is only for money, part of the Ercoli fortune? They will soon learn what you are, so don't get too settled here, Serena, will you?"

"That will do, Lucia. Serena will be a guest in my home for as long as she pleases." The old man's face was dark with anger, and for a moment Lucia wondered if she'd gone too far.

Sitting beside her mother-in-law, Serena tried to cover her distress at Lucia's ugly outburst. Above all, she didn't want her young son to hear all this! Quietly she asked her mother-in-law, "Shall we be seeing Roberto, Nonna?"

"Maybe. He is always so busy up there — " Her nod indicated the distant hills. "Or travelling to sell the wines. We don't see enough of Roberto." It was clear she missed her son; had she missed Gino as much, Serena pondered?

But to her surprise, during the conversation over dinner, she gathered that Gino had visited the Casa d'Ercoli regularly during all the years of their marriage. How then had he managed to conceal it for so long? She kept her eyes on her plate, but the bitterness in her throat made it hard to swallow the beautifully cooked meal.

She had been disconcerted too to discover that the young Maria Donati had been a close friend of his. Watching the familiar way the young girl treated the family, she wondered just how close she'd been to her husband.

After dinner, Enzo brought them coffee and liqueurs into the lounge, but after the wines she had enjoyed during the meal, Serena refused the Tia Maria he offered her with her coffee. Nicky was served the usual iced lemon drink, but child-like he pointed out to his grandmother, "I like Coke better, Nonna."

"Then Enzo shall get some for you, *caro, domani.*"

At that, Lucia Ercoli's lips curled, her eyes cold.

"You will soon spoil him, Mama."

"I have many years to make up, Lucia. Do not deny me, *cara.*" Her mother's voice was firm, and Lucia shrugged her narrow shoulders, turning to her father for support. He said, "Do not worry, *mia figlia*, I shall see that Nico is not spoilt. He must grow up a true Ercoli, to take Gino's place."

Again Nicky's dark eyes sought his mother's, not sure that he liked what he heard Nonno say. Hoping to keep the peace, Serena gave him a slight shake of her head.

★ ★ ★

"Can I sleep in here with you, Mum?"

"Why pet? Your room's lovely, you said so . . . "

"I know, but . . . " Suddenly he looked just what he was — a small boy

170

in a strange place, wanting to be near his mother. But she knew this would soon pass and she hardened her heart to the plea in those big eyes.

"Come on, Nicky, I'll read to you. Where's your book?"

As she rifled through his toys, she tried hard not to think how small he looked in the huge old bed.

Later as she lay in her own bed, she kept thinking of her sister-in-law's enmity and how her hatred could affect Nicky. I won't leave them together, she vowed silently. And then her thoughts moved to Roberto — would he resent her son as much? And as she remembered her brother-in-law's handsome face, his tall proud figure, her heart skipped a beat. As she thumped her pillow, she knew she still had her hardest hurdle to come yet.

★ ★ ★

"I saw some children in the garden, Mum. Can I go out to play with

171

them?" Serena and Nicky had eaten their croissants alone in the small breakfast-room; the grandparents were still upstairs.

"Of course, pet. But don't make too much noise, others are still in bed."

With a quick grin, he clambered down and ran through the conservatory and out into the garden as the old butler came in from the kitchens.

"Who are the children, Enzo, out there in the garden?"

"*Bambini*? Ah, they belong to the cook and to the kitchen maid. They play here while mothers work. Nico will be safe with them, *signora*."

But when old Franco Ercoli came down later, helped by the swarthy manservant who acted as his valet, he seemed rather put out that his grandson wasn't there to greet him.

"Those *ragazzi*! He should not be with them. They may have germs, bad habits — he will catch them." Angrily striving to express himself in English, he obviously didn't want Nicky mixing with the servants' children.

This was something Serena had never met before. Italians usually mixed so freely, so happily, with everyone. But of course this was her first time with one of the *nobiltà* of Italian winegrowers!

Quietly she turned to the proud old man.

"He's only a small child, Nonno. He needs other children to play with. Grown-up talk soon bores a little boy, *capisco*?" But she crossed over and called Nicky from the garden. The sun was already warm and the perfume of the flowers, the beauty of the lake made her reluctant to fetch him indoors.

"Come and say hello to your grandparents, darling." Just for a moment it looked as if he was going to protest. Then he ran indoors and went up to his grandfather and kissed his cheek.

"*Ciao*, Nonno. *Come sta?*"

"*Bene, bene*, Nico. Those children should not be in the garden. They are not suitable for you to mix with."

173

"But, Nonno . . . " Nicky began, but before he could protest further, his grandmother reached out and touched his shoulder.

"Come, Nico. I'll show you my garden. I have all kinds of secret places out there."

"Can I come too?" Serena asked, wanting to get away from the haughty old man. Fancy forbidding Nicky to play with those children!

However, she and Nicky spent a pleasant hour going round the vast gardens. Ariana Ercoli showed him a mother ladybird and a tiny bird's nest filled with speckled blue eggs.

"Soon there will be little ones, *caro*. Come, we'll see if we can find the old . . . what do you call him — the toad, *si*. He's lived in the pool for a long time."

Nicky was delighted by the sight of the big goldfish swimming amongst the pale pink water lilies. The toad didn't show, but a lazy old tortoise did, much to his surprise.

"That was Gino's pet," Nonna whispered to Serena. "Now his son plays with it! That is good, *si*?"

"Yes. I'm so glad now that I brought him to see you, *suocera*. I wish it could have been earlier . . . " Serena broke off, loath to upset her mother-in-law.

The old lady sighed and shook her head sadly.

"I shall never understand why Gino acted so. Roberto and Lucia will tell me nothing of what they found out in England. They seem to blame you, but I don't think as they do, *cara*." She turned and gave her a sweet gentle smile. Before Serena could say anything else, they were interrupted by Lucia's harsh voice.

"There you are, Madre. Cook wants to see you." And in the days that followed, Serena found Lucia always coming between her getting to know her parents-in-law better. Every time she was talking comfortably with them, Lucia found some excuse to intercede. She was even worse when they were

175

chatting to Nicky, and Serena was getting fed up of her sharp tongue, her snide remarks.

She worried too of how this was affecting Nicky. He would watch his aunt with troubled eyes, almost as if he was afraid of her. To get him away from the situation, she announced at dinner one night, "I'd like to take Nicky out for the day tomorrow — further along the lake." Nicky's face lit up, but she saw old Franco frown disapprovingly.

Later when she was taking Nicky up to bed they passed Enzo carrying a tray to the kitchens.

"I hear you say you take *piccolo* out tomorrow? It is *molto bello* in Garda, *signora*. Not far and there is a market there *domani*."

"Oh, thank you, Enzo. We'd like to see that." He gave her a wide smile and then shuffled off to the kitchens, leaving Serena feeling that in the old servant she had one friend at the Casa d'Ercoli.

Nicky didn't want to go to bed and

tried a few of his old delaying tactics.

"Come and look out, Mum. You can just see the lake from the corner of my little balcony. Come and see . . . "

"Just for a minute, and then . . . " Suddenly, as she spoke, there came the sound of crashing masonry, a grinding of metal, Nicky's cry of alarm! She flew across to the long glass window and instinctively made a grab for him.

To her horror, she saw that the left-hand side of the wrought-iron balcony had come away from the wall and was hanging down dangerously over the drop to the granite path below.

She pulled her son inside, her knees shaking with shock. Oh God, he could have been killed! As it was, he was badly shaken, his face pale, his bottom lip trembling.

"I didn't touch it, Mum, honestly! It just all broke when I walked out there." Clutching his mother's skirt, he said solemnly, "I could have fallen down there. Mum — I don't like Italy very much. I'm always falling . . . "

Still holding him close, she sat down with him on his bed, smoothing the tumble of dark curls and trying to still the clamour of her heavy heartbeat. Nicky was right; he seemed to be very accident-prone since they'd left home. Hurriedly she strove to allay his fears.

"I expect this is rather an old place, pet. They'll mend it soon while we're out I expect." And she began to tell him about tomorrow's trip.

"I'll give you some lire of your own to spend in the market, shall I?" She stayed with him until his eyes gradually closed for he was reluctant to leave go of her hand.

When she was certain he was asleep, she crossed over to the long window. The right-hand side of the balcony looked safe enough, but she tested it carefully, one foot at a time. She wanted to see for herself what had happened, didn't she? And when she did, she swallowed hard against the cry that rose to her lips. For the masonry around the socket holding the railing had been definitely gouged away!

This was no ordinary wear and tear over the years, but a deliberate attempt at making the balcony unsafe! Like a cold, dark cloud the realization chilled her to the bone. Someone had tried to kill her son! She clasped her hand over her mouth to still the moan — Nicky mustn't know.

Quietly she left and went to her own room. She sat staring into space, not wanting to believe; but it was all too clear. Somebody had purposely scraped away at the wall socket, leaving that corner of the balcony a death trap. A death trap for her little son. Hugging her arms across her chest, she rocked back and forth, a chill feeling of utter desolation deep inside her.

Shivering, she began to pace quietly up and down the room. What should she do? Had she made a mistake? Perhaps someone was repairing it; should she tell her parents-in-law about her fears? In the cold, clear light of day, it would probably sound ludicrous, wouldn't it?

Then she remembered Enzo, the old butler — she would tell him. Swiftly she hurried downstairs, through the heavy baize door and into the kitchen where he sat at a well-scrubbed table eating his dinner. Surprised to see her, he stumbled to his feet, and led her away from where the other maids were stacking away the dishes.

"Signora, cosa c'e? What happens?"

"I'm sorry to interrupt your meal, Enzo, but I'm very worried." With a typical shrug he dismissed his meal and led her to a chair.

"It's a little balcony, outside Nicky's window," she began breathlessly. "As he went out on to it tonight, one corner broke away. I just stopped him from falling. Oh Enzo, he could have been killed."

The old man drew a deep breath, his face suddenly pale beneath the years of tan. Serena put out her hand, anxious that he should believe her, understand her fears.

"I looked at it after he fell asleep. Somebody has loosened the wrought-iron rail; made the socket holding it loose."

"*Madra mia*, it is as I feared," he muttered to himself, and then, as if remembering who he was and who Serena was, he said more calmly, "I will attend to it, *signora*, tell them to mend it, make it safe for the little one."

"But who . . . " she began, but he held up his wrinkled hand.

"This place is many years old, Signora; things break away sometimes."

Biting her lip, she rose, feeling tired and still worried.

"Very well, Enzo, I'll leave it to you," and her voice showed that she was far from satisfied. And the old servant's eyes were troubled as they watched her go.

The next morning, she was glad to see that Nicky was no worse for the incident and, in fact, seemed to have forgotten it. All the same, she was thankful that they breakfasted alone and that they were going out for the day.

"I've had your car filled with *benzina, signora*. It waits for you outside. Please — *prenda cura* — take care."

"I will, Enzo, thank you." As she turned to go to the car, he called her back. "*Scusi*, I forget to give you this letter. It is for you; it came with the post for the casa this morning.

Delighted, Serena recognized Lettie's handwriting.

"*Grazie, grazie.*" She hurried to the car, leaving Nicky to look for the tortoise. Eagerly she tore open the envelope, to find there was another letter enclosed with Lettie's note.

I would not tell Danielle your address when she phoned. Told her I would enclose it with one of mine. I hope all is well with you, love. Walter and I are getting along fine. Drop me a line when you have time.

A feeling of homesickness tightened in her throat as she tore open the letter from Danielle. To her disgust, nothing was said of her abortion — no regrets and no word of repaying the loan! Instead the letter was full of her planned trip to France with a mixed group of friends who were renting a *gite* for several weeks. It was so typical of her sister; she tore it up in disgust, and went to call Nicky. It was time they were on their way.

6

THE journey from Bardolino to Garda didn't take long. It was still rather early for the height of the tourist trade, although Serena found the main street in Garda busy with the local shopkeepers' trucks taking their wares to the hotels clustered along the lake.

"Let's park the car, shall we?"

Winding down the window, she leaned out to ask a broad-shouldered young lorry driver where she could safely do so. His dark eyes lit with admiration at the sight of the fair-haired young woman, and he offered to take her — to show her and maybe take a *cappuccino*? She was getting used to the blatant fulsome glances of the Italian males of all ages. In fact, it was beginning to make her feel one hundred per cent female!

"No, *grazie*, just direct me and I will find it." Not at all rebuffed, the flirtatious young man told her to use the car-park alongside the small bus station up the road.

"Grazie, signor."

"Prego." With a cheeky grin, he kissed his fingertips in her direction. *"Bellissima, signorina."*

To her amusement she saw Nicky give him a black look. He was getting very protective of his mother! After parking the car, they began to wander through the cobbled alleyways, under old stone arches, fascinated by the noise and bustle and charm of the various shops. Colourful fresh fruit and vegetables; white marble slabs with strange-looking fish; beautiful clothes and the soft leather of the finest footwear in the world. It was all there, along with the aromas of cooking, the wonderful smell of coffee. And everywhere excitable voluble Italians, straw bags overflowing with their purchases, or sitting in the sun in the little piazzas.

Nicky loved it and Serena couldn't help notice that he grew more Italian with every passing day. One thing he didn't like was the fuss they made of him; stopping to kiss his cheeks soundly, exclaiming over and over,

"Bello. Bello ragazzo." His face would go red, his dark brows frowning with embarrassment.

"Don't worry, pet. It's nice when everybody likes you."

He rubbed his cheek with the back of his hand. "Not when they kiss you all the time," he grumbled.

"Let's get a drink, shall we?" But once inside the little café, he caught sight of the *gelato* bar with at least a dozen different coloured ice-creams on offer. Patiently Serena waited while he tried to decide which flavour he wanted. To his delight, the tubby little proprietor gave him a scoop of several kinds and then refused to let him pay for them. She was to come across this often; the child-loving Latins simply spoilt him rotten!

"Oh *grazie, signor.*"

"Prego, bambino, prego."

"I want to see the lake, Mum."

"Come on then, pet." Gathering up her bag and cardigan, she suddenly noticed a tall thin man sitting at a table near the door. His face and figure seemed somehow familiar. Surely she'd seen him before — more than once! On the plane and again in Venice? No, she couldn't be right, could she? She found that so many Italians looked alike, yet this man was taller than most. She shrugged and walked past him, her eyes averted. After all, it could be just a coincidence, couldn't it?

Just round the corner of a picturesque hotel, they could see the lake, a vivid azure blue in the sunlight.

"Isn't it big, Mum, like the sea? And look at all the boats!" At a long wooden landing stage near them, one of the lake steamers was just taking on passengers, while further out they could see the white wash of a powerful hydrofoil. On the far side of the lake the road passed through tunnels cut out of the rocky mountainside. And in the distance were the tall walls of an old castle and another little town.

"Here, look, Mum, I can see hundreds of fishes. Look here."

Once more Serena clutched the back of his T-shirt to prevent another ducking. The lake water was so transparent they could clearly see shoals of tiny silver fishes. Men were sitting in boats and on the end of landing stages contentedly smoking watching as their floats bobbed idly on the surface of the water.

Restaurants and cafés had their tables and chairs spread out right down to the water's edge. Gay check cloths, little lamps and candles that would light up the promenade at night, tubs of flowers, everywhere bright flowers, with vine-covered pergolas giving some shade in the bright sunlight. All so beautiful against the backcloth of the sparkling lake that Serena caught her breath. Surely this must be one of Italy's loveliest places; sheltered on one side by mountains, with green hills and vineyards on the other.

"Can we go on a boat?" Nicky urged excitedly.

"Another day, pet. We've got plenty of time. We could go all round the lake. There's a lot of other little towns all round. We could come out and have dinner one night, outside, near the water."

"Promise?"

"Scout's honour." She crossed her heart with one hand and squeezed Nicky's with the other. "Now let's find this market, shall we?"

This time she asked a *poliziotto*, who gave her the direction and touched his cap smartly as she thanked him. It seemed from what he said that this market moved on, setting up at a different place round the lake each day. It stretched for at least half a mile along the lakeside promenade. The stalls were selling every kind of article. Sweet stalls with pink and white nougat bars; fruit stalls ablaze with colour. Clothes at amazingly low prices and good quality; shoes, toys, the choice was endless.

The noise, bustle and chatter filled the air with a festive feeling of holiday time. It was the beautiful pottery stalls that caught their eye, delighting them the most. Brilliant red, deep blues, pristine white, and always the lovely local terracotta urns looking still the same as in the days of the Romans.

"We can't take that home, love, it's too heavy!" Nicky had his father's eye for beauty, and Serena had a job persuading him not to buy. They settled finally on an elegant deep-blue fruit bowl made of delicately intertwined strips of china as a present for Lettie.

For lunch, they found a table on the very edge of the water so that Nicky could watch the boats. All around families were enjoying the delicious food, the local wines. Serena raised her face to the sun; she was getting a nice apricot-tinted tan, whilst Nicky's olive skin seemed to deepen with each passing day.

Leisurely taking their time, they finally ordered a soup — *crema di pollo*, a luscious ravioli to follow and with the restaurant's speciality as a sweet — a sort of *tortiglione* — an almond cake that Nicky adored. Serena had a half carafe of the pale dry Soave wine, one of her favourites, while Nicky had his usual Coke in a long-stemmed frosted glass. All this made him feel very grown-up and she added to this by letting him pay the bill and tip the smiling waiter.

"Can we see some more of the market, Mum?"

"Just a little. My poor feet are killing me!"

"I want to buy some more of that nougat for those children I saw in the garden." Should she remind him of his grandfather's displeasure about playing with those children, she wondered, and then decided not to. After all, it was

191

good that he should spend his pocket money this way, wasn't it?

Again the stallholder gave him a wide smile and an extra bar of nougat as Nicky carefully counted out the lire and accepted the gift-wrapped packet.

"I'm going to sit in the sun for a while on this seat; don't go too far away, pet, will you?"

"No, I won't," he assured her and then ran off to where a group of little boys were bending over various containers of fish. In no time at all, he was one of them, accepting the loan of a small fishing rod, hooking a worm and casting off as if he'd always fished there.

She heard his cry of delight as he caught one, and his dark head joined the others leaning excitedly over an old bucket. The sun made her feel drowsy but she daren't risk dropping off to sleep. She felt that she had to watch him all the time, but she was loath to move.

"Come on, Nicky," she called.

Reluctantly he shrugged and then waving his goodbyes, he came back.

"Oh, Mum, we were having such a good time."

"I know, love, but it's time to get back. Let's have a milkshake first though. You choose."

The long after-lunch siesta over, the shops were beginning to open again and the traffic thickened as they drove back to the Casa d'Ercoli.

"It was smashing there, Mum." Nicky wriggled contentedly in his seat.

"Smashing!" she agreed with a smile, hoping that Lucia was in a good mood for once when they got back. There was something about her sister-in-law that worried her. She often caught her looking at Nicky with positive dislike in her cold eyes.

I'll never forgive her for suggesting that they thought Gino had picked me up as a prostitute, she told herself heatedly.

★ ★ ★

"Look, Nonno, I've bought a present for Lettie." Clutching his parcels, Nicky ran through to the conservatory expecting to see his grandfather out there as usual.

But as a tall, dark man rose from the lounger, he stopped, his little face suddenly ashen.

"Papa . . . ?" he choked as he reached forward, only to stop, his eyes huge and tear-filled as they saw that this man was not Gino, but someone so like — and yet unlike?

The little boy's shoulders sagged and he turned his bewildered face to his mother.

"It's not . . . I thought it was Papa," he whispered. Swiftly she knelt down beside him, her arms holding him close, sharing his grief.

"I know, *caro*, I know. This is Papa's older brother." Her throat ached as she strove to hold back her own tears. And as she looked up at him, the man seemed to tower over her like a dark shadow.

"*Ciao*, Nico. I am your *zio* — your uncle, Roberto." The voice, so like his father's, made Nicky look up, his eyes searching, his bottom lip still trembling. Then, after a long assessing look, he held out a small hand.

"*Molto lieto, Zio*?" The formal reply was not lost on Serena, and pride in her young son warmed her heart. "How do you do, Uncle?"

Roberto's lips thinned, but he answered, "The grandparents are out, Nico. Can I see Lettie's present?"

"You don't know Lettie!"

"I did meet her; you too."

Disbelief in his voice, Nicky said stubbornly, "No! I don't remember you at all." And at that moment, his firm chin was very like his uncle's.

"But I remember you, *piccolo*. You were asleep when I called. I met your Lettie then too."

"Oh." Still doubtful, Nicky gave him a faint smile and then carefully unwrapped the dish.

"*Bello, bello*. She will like that very much, Nico. Especially if you bought it with your own money."

"I did," Nicky assured him proudly.

"And this other . . . ?"

"It's nougat. I bought it for the children I played with out there in the garden. But Nonno sent them away. I thought they'd play with me again if I gave them the nougat."

Seeing the puzzled look cross Roberto's face, Serena added softly, "The servants' children."

"Ah," he answered slowly, "I see." He had understood at once, but to her surprise, he told Nicky, "I'm sure they will. In fact, I'll tell them to come again soon, shall I?"

This time he was rewarded by a wide smile from his nephew.

"*Grazie, Zio, grazie.*"

"Come." With an arm round the small shoulders, Roberto led Nicky to his seat. "Tell me, how are you liking your first time in Italy, Nico?"

"Smashing. We had a great time today in Garda, didn't we, Mum?"

"And the Casa d'Ercoli? You like it here?"

For a moment Nicky pondered, giving the question some thought. "It's OK, I guess, but it's very old. My balcony broke and I nearly fell. Mum was scared, but I wasn't."

"Balcony?" His uncle's thick brows made a dark question mark as he looked across at Serena.

"Er — the wrought-iron railing came away from the wall and the left-hand side of the balcony tipped. I caught Nicky just in time. I'd like to discuss it with you some other time." Her green eyes flashed in Nicky's direction, their message clear. She didn't want him to hear what she had to say!

"I really wanted to go on a boat, and to see the grapes growing," Nicky added. "I've never seen them growing back home."

"Well, *mio nipote*, I can fix both of those for you. We all go up to the vineyards next week. As for the boat, I have one in the boathouse. You shall take a trip with me."

"Your own boat? One that goes fast?" Excitedly, Nicky soon had his uncle describing his boat to him. As she watched them, Serena's thoughts were troubled. Should she risk letting Roberto take her son anywhere? Surely all those accidents were not all coincidences — the car, the fall into the canal in Venice, the balcony?

She threaded her fingers through her thick hair; was she imagining it all? Was it just that, like many small boys, he was accident-prone? She was certain though that she didn't imagine all those dark looks Lucia gave him! And what if Roberto too resented another heir to the Ercoli fortune? If so, she thought, seeing how well he and Nicky were getting on together, then he didn't make it as obvious as his sister.

"Can we, Mum?" With a start she heard Nicky's question.

"Can we what, pet?"

"Go in Uncle Roberto's boat tomorrow?"

Seeing her hesitation, her doubtful look in her eyes, Roberto added his plea. "You'll be quite safe, *mia cognata*. It's a beautiful boat." There was something in his voice, a quirk round his sensuous mouth that taunted her. Had he been reading her mind; did he suspect that she was afraid to trust him with her son?

"Please, Mum, say we can."

"Of course, pet. I'll go as well. Thank you, Roberto." But his expression was remote, unreadable, his smile cool.

"*Prego*, we'll go early in the morning before it gets too hot then." And with that he went on chatting to Nicky who began telling him about the boats they saw on the Thames.

* * *

After dinner that night, after she'd finished her coffee and liqueur, Roberto rose and held out his hand.

"Come and take a stroll in the garden with me, Serena, we have much to say, *si*?" For a moment, she wanted to refuse, and then seeing a challenge in his eyes, she rose and followed him through the long glass doors.

It was a beautiful evening. The sky, navy-blue and cloudless, was full of stars; stars that looked so near you could almost reach up to touch them. The air was still warm and fragrant with the smell of flowers all around them; the tinkle of the little fountains the only sound.

To her consternation, she was terribly conscious of the tall figure at her side; conscious of the faint aroma of expensive aftershave, his thin dark cigar. And something else — a male, almost animal-like smell that invaded her senses and set her heart beating faster.

"It's so lovely out here." She lifted her face to the moonlit sky, almost afraid to disturb the silence between them. He stopped and looked down intently into her face, his dark eyes searching it as if he was trying to discover something, some truth he wasn't sure of.

"I think we were all wrong about you, Serena." His voice was quiet, solemn. "I wanted you out here to myself so that I could apologize to you."

As she made to demur, he held up his hand.

"No, please, let me go on." He drew in a deep breath and then went on slowly, "Yes, we were so wrong. When we — I learned from the London office of Gino's marriage, realized he'd never told us in all those years, we thought the worst of the woman he had kept hidden from us all. Thought she wasn't suitable to meet us. Then," again he paused and his voice thickened as he began to say, "I found out about his way of life in England — all the girls he had — more and more, including the one who died in the car crash with him . . ."

As they walked slowly along the path, the flowering shrubs brushing their shoulders, Serena was tempted to tell him too about Danielle and how Gino had left her pregnant before he moved on to the dead girl. But why soil Gino's name further; give his family more grief and worry? So she decided to keep it to herself.

"Then I said those awful things to you. I am deeply sorry, I was wrong. Why, I even thought the boy might not be Gino's until I saw him there asleep — so like him." He stopped and turned to her. "Please, say you will forgive me — us, for what we so wrongly thought. For what I said, and above all, Serena, for how my brother treated you. If only I had known." Anger trembled in his voice and the look on his face made her shiver. "He was a fool, a stupid fool."

"It's all in the past now, Roberto. So please, let's try to forget it. I'm going to." And she turned away not wanting him to see how it affected her.

"You must stay here now and live with us, as one of the Ercoli family."

At that, her empathy faded. "Stay here? But I can't, I have my work, Lettie, my home. And Nicky's school . . . oh no, we can't stay here. I meant this as a visit, that's all!"

"But Nico should be one of us now. There are no other children yet to inherit, *capisco*?"

"You and Lucia are both still young enough to have a family," she insisted. And as she spoke, she wondered why this good-looking man was still not married. He must be about thirty-five or so.

He shrugged as if dismissing her words as nothing.

"Then you should leave him here with us if you wish to return to London."

The cool effrontery of this man made her fury boil over.

"Certainly not! He's far too young to lose his mother too. I'd never leave my son, never." The rising anger nearly choked her and suddenly all the softness, the beauty of the night fell away. How dare they presume she would hand over her child to them! Her breast rose and fell as she drew in a deep breath. She was about to burst out and tell him too of her fear for Nicky's safety, but just in time, she bit her lip to hold back the words.

Suppose her fears were groundless, the incidents purely accidental? But if they weren't and what if Roberto disliked Nicky as much as Lucia did, but was cleverer at disguising it?

The thoughts whirled round in her head and she felt so alone. Her slim shoulders sagged and she longed for Lettie's calm common sense, for old Walter's kindly support. Here she felt as if she was in an enemy camp!

Roberto touched her arm. "Please Serena, let us not quarrel. Stay as long as you can; all may be resolved by the time you go."

Before she could answer, he changed the subject.

"Is there any special place round the lake you wish to see tomorrow? My boat is yours to command," he finished with a mock bow. With an effort she tried to go along with him.

"Anywhere, Roberto, it all looks so lovely."

He smiled and as he did, she wished he smiled more often for it softened his proud features and made him seem younger, more approachable.

When they returned to the villa, he began to tell his parents of the proposed boat trip in the morning. And as he did, something made Serena glance quickly across at Lucia. What she saw on her face made a cold tremor surge through her veins.

★ ★ ★

The sun was already casting its rays of light through the soft mist shrouding the water's edge when they went down to the old boathouse at the bottom end of the garden. Smelling of tar and rope and paint, it was gloomy in there until Roberto propped open both of the big doors.

Nicky couldn't take in everything quickly enough. And then as the whole place lightened, they could see the boat gently rocking there.

"Oh Mum, isn't it great?" Painted blue and white, with all its rails gleaming in the early sun, it looked big and powerful, taking up the whole space.

"I have had it all made ready. There is food and water enough in the galley. This way." Roberto's pride in the craft was obvious. The gap in the rail already held the narrow gangplank and he helped Serena aboard and then Nicky, taking their gear down below.

After much consideration, she had dressed in white cotton pants with a black and white top. She was being very careful not to upset her in-laws by wearing bright colours for she knew how firmly the Italians adhered to black for mourning. However, she didn't mind, for she knew that black suited her fair colouring. In the sunlight her hair gleamed like molten silver and Roberto, adjusting the controls, found his eyes constantly drawn to its shining glory.

The engine exploded into life and the noise echoed round the boathouse and then settled down to a powerful hum. Sitting on the seat that ran round the wheel deck, she couldn't help but admire the sight of his tall figure, his firm hand busy first with the controls and then the wheel. He was all in white emphasizing his dark colouring to perfection.

Slowly he inched the powerful boat out into the shallow water, and passing their small landing stage, he swung it out into the blue lake. At once the wind caught Serena's hair and she tied a chiffon scarf round it to keep it out of her eyes. Nicky, his face alight with glee, held it up as the wind tossed his dark curls awry. But Roberto reached into a small compartment and pulled a cap firmly over one eye, making him look like a pirate, she thought.

Already the lake was getting busy with craft of all kinds; steamers loaded with sightseeing tourists; small rowing boats of hopeful fishermen, vendors carrying goods to the local hotels, even some small yachts, sails bright in the sun. Chattering waiters were setting out the tables and chairs on the newly swept promenade; cats sat preening on the rails, while the dark-skinned local women did their shopping and the men collected their newspapers. The whole kaleidoscope of brilliant colour and movement filled Serena with pleasure.

"We'll pass Garda as you've already seen that. If we have time, we'll swim in the lake there on the way back, shall we?" Roberto suggested to Nicky.

"Yes, please. Look, I've got my new swim trunks on underneath," the boy pointed out and Serena saw his uncle smile as he looked down at the tiny briefs. She had also put a bikini under her pants.

"Can I drive, please, Uncle?" Still smiling, Roberto put the small hands on the wheel, covering them with his own, gently helping Nicky to steer.

The look of sheer delight on her son's face brought a lump to her throat; he'd been missing a father — a man in his life, hadn't he? Turning to her, Roberto asked, "Shall we dock here at Malcesine, Serena? I think you'll like it here." As she nodded her assent, he took over the wheel, slowing down between the cluster of boats in the quaint little harbour and they clambered ashore.

Taking a deep breath, she stood looking around, utterly charmed by the picture before her. A tall, medieval castle towered over a cluster of cream and yellow houses at the lakeside and behind it all rose an impressive looking mountain.

"Scaliger Castle," Roberto pointed out, "and there is Monte Baldo. Come." Taking Nicky's small hand in his, he led them up and away from the harbour, through cobblestone alleyways. "We'll have coffee here, shall we?"

The little bars and cafes were all open now and busy. Serena and Nicky couldn't resist the jumble of shops, especially those selling toys. His uncle watched as Nicky played with a little monkey on a stick, carved locally no doubt during the slack winter months.

"You like that, *piccolo*?"

"Yes, he's funny — watch." And Nicky made the little monkey climb the stick, then turn over and tumble down again.

"Here, go buy it, *si*?" Roberto thrust a lire note into his nephew's willing hand with a smile.

"You'll spoil him."

He turned dark serious eyes to hers as he replied, using the same words his mother had used before, "I have many years to make up."

"Of course. I'm sorry."

"Non ha importanza." He shrugged and she felt rebuffed at the cool reply.

Turning away, she glanced unseeingly into the next shop window, her face flushed.

Nicky joined them, happily clutching his toy and the change.

"Thank you, Zio, *grazie*."

"*Prego*. Now something for *suo madre, si?*"

"Yes, please! Oh look, she hasn't got a fan. They're very pretty Uncle Roberto, aren't they?" Indeed the window that Serena had been staring in so blindly was full of beautiful fans of all colours and sizes.

"Er — no! Oh Nicky, you shouldn't . . . " she broke off nervously at the thunderous look on the man's face.

"Come," he ordered taking her arm and propelling her into the shop. "Shall you choose or I?"

Flustered she glanced around, bewildered by the sight of so many gorgeous fans; the prices made her flinch.

"A black one, please." Without really choosing, she pointed out one that looked the least expensive.

"No, something better," he nodded to the all-too-willing assistant, "in black."

And they finally came out with the most expensive black fan in the shop! Of gorgeous lace, it had tiny coloured stones set in the ebony ribs; opened out it looked like a glorious peacock. In spite of her qualms, Serena adored it on sight, while Nicky fully approved and said so loudly.

"Oh, thank you, Roberto, *grazie*," she breathed. "It's lovely."

At that moment so was she, the man thought, with her greeny/blue eyes shining up at him like stars.

"My pleasure, *signora*," he smiled, again with a mock bow and it crossed Serena's mind that, just then, they must look like a happy family, enjoying the day out.

All the same, he chose a sedate hotel café for their coffee. She knew Nicky would have preferred one of the little outside ones where he could watch the lake. And instead of a cone, he had to sit eating his ice-cream from an elegant glass dish. The fragrant coffee from a tall silver pot was wonderful, but she felt nervous as she poured it out, feeling Roberto watching her as she did so.

What was it about this man that affected her so? she thought as they slowly made their way back to the boat.

"We'll make for Riva now, shall we?" Serena, sitting on the bench seat near the wheel, had been day-dreaming, her face lifted to the sun and at the sound of his voice turned bemused eyes to his.

"Riva?" he repeated. "The most northern point of the lake. Very good climate even with the Dolomites behind it."

Alert now, he pointed out the tall tower coming into view.

"La Rocca Castle — what's left of it. Built in the twelfth century. Lots of medieval buildings and some of the

Roman wall still remains in Riva."

She could tell how much he loved the lake and the little towns around it every time he spoke. It was his home, his birthright, part of his pride, his background. To her surprise, the tower was quite near to the water, surrounded by moats used as moorings. Again the ancient narrow lanes leading off this busy square were crammed with exclusive shops and restaurants. As before, they passed the crowded pavement cafés to pause before a quaint hotel, its ornately frescoed façade fronting the elegant dining-room within.

But as if he understood the disappointment on Nicky's face, Roberto told the attentive maitre d', "We will eat outside in the garden."

"*Si, signor*," and with a bow he led them through to the delightful gardens at the rear of the hotel. Vine-covered canopies created cool shade above the elegant white wrought-iron tables, many of which were already occupied. To Nicky's delight, several other small children were there dining with the grown-ups.

Patiently Roberto helped him to choose exactly what he wanted from the long, leather-bound menu.

"*A insalata di riso e scampi*, please Uncle. And *zuppa inglese* for pudding." Nicky couldn't read well enough yet, but Serena was surprised how willingly his uncle guided his choice.

"I'll just have the rice and scampi salad too, please, Roberto. No sweet — or perhaps a little cheese to finish."

"And the wine?" He raised dark eyebrows in query.

"You choose."

Of course he began with a pasta dish. It always amazed her how the Italians kept so slim whilst eating such mounds of pasta before the main course. The light white wine was made locally and was cool and refreshing to the palate. As they lingered over the fragrant coffee, Roberto excused his young nephew, who ran to join the other children playing round a splashing old fountain.

"Nicky never speaks of his father, I notice." The sudden change in their conversation made Serena's heart skip a beat.

"He's so young — he forgets for a long time in between, and then suddenly brings it up." She was annoyed to hear the stammer in her voice. "Actually, he — we didn't see all that much of Gino. Just an odd night or day and then months of nothing. As I've told you, after Nicky's birth, we were practically separated. He had his other little 'loves' — I had my son and my job."

He raised quizzical eyes at that.

"No one else for you?"

"That's my business, Roberto," she replied coldly.

"*Mi scusi dispiace*. I'm sorry — of course it is."

She shrugged, not really believing he was sorry. A good-looking couple had finished eating and on their way out paused to speak to him. He introduced her briefly as his sister-in-law and then engaged in rapid conversation with the man.

Serena noticed that the expensively dressed young woman with him never took her eyes off Roberto and was trying hard to capture his attention. Whether he saw this or not, he treated her with cool courtesy and nothing more. Serena wondered to herself just why she was pleased to see this.

Finally with a polite bow in her direction, they made their goodbyes and left and Roberto signalled for their bill. She had a job prising young Nicky away from his new-found friends.

"We're going for a swim on the way back, darling," she promised.

"We'll go across to Limone on the other side some other time," Roberto put in. "There's so much to see there."

"I want to swim, please. I can swim without my armbands now, Uncle." Already showing signs of hero-worshipping his uncle, Nicky was keen to impress with his new skill in the water.

"*Corraggioso, piccolo*. You're a brave boy then, Nico." And the small boy's chest seemed to swell at his uncle's praise. Back on the boat, he was once more allowed a turn at the wheel. This time with his uncle's firm hands covering his small ones, he was shown how to guide the sleek craft carefully away from the moorings and into the lake.

Relaxing in the sun, her eyes half-closed against the bright sparkle from the water, Serena found it hard to keep suspecting this man of wanting to harm her son. Watching his care, seeing how well Nicky trusted him, she found herself longing to trust him completely too. Laughing at something his nephew was saying, he looked much younger, less reserved. The creases round his lips as he grinned down at Nicky, his white teeth contrasting cleanly with his deep tan, softened the proud jawline. And once again, Serena felt a sudden heat rising from the pit of her stomach — he was so handsome. As she watched him, she wondered again what it would be like to be loved by this man. He would show a different side of his character to the woman he loved, wouldn't he? She reckoned that maybe only the woman he loved would be able to manage him. A woman he loved . . . Remembering too how he'd been all day with young Nicky, she considered he'd be a wonderful father. Was she wrong in thinking he could be trying to warn her away; wanted her to leave Nicky at the Casa d'Ercoli at his mercy and that of his cold-eyed sister?

With a start, she realized that Nicky had been calling out to her and she sat up with a jerk to see Roberto watching her closely.

"You were far away, *si*? With not so pleasant thoughts maybe?" Almost as if he'd been reading her mind, she mused.

"Just lazy. How far to where we're

going to swim?" she asked to change the subject.

"I've just told you, Mum," put in Nicky impatiently, "we're nearly there."

"In that case, sailor boy, we'll go down and strip off, shall we?" But he was reluctant to leave the wheel.

"I'm going to leave my things here with Uncle Roberto's."

"Right, I won't be a moment."

Once in the cabin and divested of her slacks and top, she felt rather wary of the skimpiness of her bikini. Just three small triangles of black Lycra, it revealed so much . . .

As an afterthought, she took Nicky a pair of small rubber sandshoes for his feet.

"Do we need towels?" Both males turned at the sound of her voice.

"Wow, Mum!" Nicky grinned his delight.

Feeling the heat stain her cheeks, she glanced slowly across at the tall man beside him and her heart began to thump painfully against her ribs. For he was looking at her with naked desire dark in those compelling eyes of his. For one long moment, she saw blatant hunger reaching out towards her. And in that same long moment, she felt the same hunger burning inside her!

And then it was gone, leaving her wondering if she had imagined it — that the vibrant tension in the air was coming only from her trembling body and not his. Just in time she stopped herself wrapping her arms across her bare midriff, and when she raised her eyes once more his expression was unreadable.

Like Nicky he had shed his top clothes and his brief white swim trunks left little to the imagination. The sight of his broad tanned shoulders and slim hips made the pulse in her throat quicken. A stray lock of dark hair fell unheeded across his brow and her fingers tingled with the urge to reach out and brush it back! For a few breathless seconds, it seemed that all the years without love were now seeking some fulfilment, and every nerve in her body clamoured for the touch of this man's hands.

"Shall we need towels?" she repeated and her voice sounded breathless, so she turned and gave Nicky the rubber pumps.

"Put these on, pet: save any cuts, won't they?"

To her relief they moored alongside the long narrow ramp leading back to the bank.

"You thought we would have to dive overboard, m'm?" Again she was amazed by how easily Roberto could read her thoughts. With a wicked grin, he reached out a long finger and touched her soft cheek.

"You have such a give-away face, *cara*." And she felt the heat of that touch until they reached the little bay. Beneath the trees, large flat stones served as diving points, although just there the water was rather shallow, clear enough to see the pebbles below.

A wide barrier circled the area, acting as a filter, so that a lovely natural bathing pool had been created beside the shore.

It was full of noisy families, happily splashing around. Others sprawled on the rocks, drying out in the warm sun.

"Not much good for real swimming here, but I will watch the little one."

So will I, thought Serena, then felt troubled that she distrusted him so!

They had a wonderful time. Little Nicky was in raptures, and as he played with the small ones near the edge, Serena gave herself the pleasure of a good rapid crawl to the pool's furthest edge and back. Puffing, she surfaced — straight into a pair of strong arms.

"Roberto . . . !" Laughing, he held her close. And the feel of his long, lithe body close to hers, the tactile touch of the black hair on the broad chest pressed close to hers, made every nerve tingle with awareness.

Wicked, brilliant eyes beneath long

wet spiky lashes watched the colour rise in her cheeks.

"*Bella, cara.* You swim well, sister-in-law." She nodded, not trusting her voice, and then freeing herself from the firm grip, she looked round for Nicky.

"You must not smother the boy, Serena. He is growing up now," he called after her as she swam over to where Nicky was being splashed boisterously by a couple of bigger boys.

"Time to go, darling."

"Oh no, Mum. I'm having a smashing time here. Toni's going to teach me to dive."

"Not today, love. You've been in long enough." He grumbled all the way back to the boat. They wrung out as much water as they could, but his hair was thick and still soaking.

"If you wish to help me steer, Nico, you must first dry out this . . ." Roberto ruffled the wet mop. "There is a hair-dryer down there, go." And without a word, Nicky obeyed. He liked using his mother's dryer at home, so she left him to it and hurriedly got into her own clothes.

Then just as she was pulling her top over her head, she heard Nicky cry out — there was a flash and she heard something go phutt! And then the thud of Nicky falling . . . screaming . . .

"Roberto, here quick." Sheer terror in her voice, she rushed into the cabin.

"Oh God! Nicky . . . " He was sprawled over on to the floor, the hairdryer still sizzling beside him. His face was pale beneath his tan, his breathing shallow, and he looked so frightened.

"Mum — it went off. Oh, my arm." Big tears welled up in his scared eyes.

"Here, let me see." Roberto pushed her aside and knelt down, massaging the little boy's right arm.

"What happened, Nicky?"

Her voice was trembling with shock as Roberto put in,

"The dryer blew a fuse, I expect. Thank heavens our voltage is so low. There, is that better, Nico?"

"A bit, Zio. But it still tingles, all funny." The colour was gradually coming back to his cheeks.

"Thank goodness for those rubber shoes — he could have died." Serena was still shaking with fear. Not another accident to her precious son — or was it an accident? Had that faulty hair-dryer been meant for her?

All her doubts and fears, all the barely concealed suspicion came flooding back. Dear heavens, weren't they safe anywhere? Had Roberto planned this?

Her heart felt like lead in her breast, for she knew that deep down she didn't want it to be true; didn't want him guilty of this, another ugly mishap to Nicky.

She made her son lie on the bunk. Until they reached the Casa d'Ercoli, she would watch him carefully. As she sat there, staring misty-eyed out of the tiny porthole, she couldn't bring herself to believe Roberto could be so caring and kind one moment and yet still plan anything so wicked as giving one of them an electric shock. She shuddered again at the realization — wet hands, wet clothes, wet hair — it could have been fatal, couldn't it?

Nicky was so little. And yet, her treacherous heart insisted, it could have been just a fuse going phut! They did, often. Seeing that Nicky had dozed off to sleep, she went up to the wheel deck, leaving the cabin door open.

"Is he all right?"

"Yes, he's asleep." Her words came out flat and cold and Roberto's brow creased in query.

"It was an accident, Serena. I had the man check the boat thoroughly, but how could he have foreseen a fuse blowing like that?"

She shrugged, not wanting to voice her fears aloud, to accuse him — of what? All she could think of now was the danger to her little son. Too many coincidences added up — to something nasty. And she didn't know who to trust, did she?

I won't let his good looks fool me,

she told herself firmly. I should have learned my lesson from Gino — never to trust the Ercoli family.

And the tall dark man at her side could feel her distrust. And the sun went out of their lovely day.

They had little to say to each other for the rest of the journey back, but when Nicky awoke, he seemed little the worse for his shock.

As Roberto carefully steered the graceful craft into the boathouse, he called out to the man working at the far end.

"See me later!"

Wearily Serena gathered up their kit whilst Nicky dashed off excitedly to tell his *nonno* all about the trip. He was still chattering away during dinner that night, but something in Serena's manner made her mother-in-law ask quietly, "You did not enjoy the trip so much, *cara*?"

With a start, Serena brought her attention back to the older woman beside her.

"Er — yes, Nonna, of course I did. It was lovely . . . "

"Then why so pensive, my dear? What troubles you?"

"I had a shock," Nicky burst in then importantly, "from the hair-dryer in the cabin." And he went on to give a highly coloured description of the accident.

Oriana Ercoli gently touched Serena's arm.

"I see. Of course, you were upset. Don't worry. Roberto is very careful with his boat; it won't happen again."

Serena lowered her eyes, pushing the food around her plate. Won't it? she thought bitterly — who could she trust? Were they all as deceitful and conniving as Gino had been?

When she looked up again, she saw Roberto watching her closely, a shadow crossing his face. Beside him, his sister was also looking at her. And the set of *her* face made Serena shiver.

After dinner, she went up to put Nicky to bed, read him a story, and saw his eyes closing in sleep before she left him. He looked so small and defenceless lying there and all her love for him welled up inside her breast, making her throat ache. Dear God, if anything should happen to him — if she should lose him!

Restlessly, she couldn't face going down to the lounge to the others, so she slipped silently out into the garden. Slowly, taking in deep gulps of the soft night air, she felt her nerves grow calmer.

She tried to reason with her fears. After all she was probably quite over-protective of her child, she told herself as she strolled slowly amongst the flowering shrubs, the night-scented stocks.

"So here you are, *cara*." Startled, she swung round. She hadn't heard Roberto's approach; he moves like some sleek animal, she thought.

"Hello, Roberto. I — I just needed a few minutes alone . . . "

"Shall I leave you then, sister-in-law?"

A hint of challenge in his voice made her say hurriedly, "Of course not." For a while they moved side by side beneath the vine-covered pergola arches.

"Tell me . . . " he asked quietly.

"Tell you what?" She paused, turning to look up at him. But just then a small cloud covered the moon and she saw only the dark outline of his face.

"Tell me what is worrying you, Serena. I could see that those troubled thoughts of yours were bothering you all through dinner."

"I was thinking about that electric shock Nicky got today, and the balcony giving way." The words came tumbling out before she could stop them.

"The hair-dryer . . . " — she felt him shrug beside her — "a fuse. Happens all the time in Italy." His amused dismissal of the accident angered her then.

"But the balcony . . . ?"

"Listen, Serena. Every year when we all go up to the vineyard, the workmen move in and do any necessary repairs, alterations, redecorating and so on. This week they are looking round, marking out, making notes." He paused and then went on, "That is probably what has happened. Somebody scraped away the mortar to see the extent of the damage. Nicky should not have been given that room, or the door to the balcony should have been kept locked. They slipped up there — didn't tell us. They perhaps didn't know he was in that room."

Still she didn't answer and his voice held a tinge of exasperation as he added, "It's a large place, *cara*, sometimes mistakes are made." He reached out just as the moon appeared again from behind the cloud and held her shoulders tightly.

"You don't believe me, do you, Serena? You think all the Ercoli men are like Gino — liars?"

"I don't know. I don't know what to think." There was such a depth of uncertainty, of loneliness in her voice then that he slipped his arms around her slender waist and pulled her close.

"*Povera piccina* — poor little one." His voice was husky and she found comfort in the warmth of his arms, his nearness. "You must trust me, *cara*," he murmured into the scent of her hair.

Trust him? She pushed him away, not wanting to be dazzled by the attraction she felt for this man.

"I'm going in, Roberto. Thank you for today." And with that she turned and hurried back to the house.

7

"I THOUGHT I was going up to see the grapes growing soon," Nicky asked rather petulantly the following week.

"So did I, love, but Uncle Roberto said we have to wait. It seems the crop's a bit late this year. Don't worry, Nicky, we'll be going soon." Like her son, Serena was looking forward to the move up to the vineyard.

It was getting warmer each day round the lake, and more tourists arrived every week. But most of all she wanted to get away from Roberto. Once they started working on the grape vines, he would be busy and she wouldn't need to try so hard to avoid him. Hopefully too, she would see less of the po-faced Lucia who still never let an opportunity pass to sneer at her and find fault with Nicky.

The young Maria Donati was very friendly with Lucia who seemed to encourage the girl's obvious pursuit of Roberto.

"I don't know why Maria dislikes me so, Nonna, do you?" Serena was helping her mother-in-law to sort out her skeins of embroidery silks. There was a cool breeze coming up the garden, and for a while the conservatory was a pleasant place to sit. Remembering Maria's rudeness that morning, she hoped Oriana could tell her what she was supposed to have done wrong.

The old lady went on stranding her silks, her face taut for a moment. Then with a sigh, she glanced up at her daughter-in-law, a hint of pity in her blue eyes.

"She was to marry Gino! These last few years, he was waiting for her to grow up." She paused and her lips thinned. "It was to be an arranged marriage, as so many here still are. Her family and ours have been linked in business for years."

Serena drew in a deep breath at the shocked dismay that swept through her at Nonna's revelation! Was she never to know the end of Gino's duplicity?

"Maria is not to blame. She, like all of us, did not know of your marriage to Gino. He — he still courted her on his visits here. When Roberto told her the truth, she was mortified, ashamed somehow. He was so kind to her, and now she clings to him." The old lady shrugged as if the actions of the younger generation were beyond her comprehension. "And since then, she seems to have transferred her affections to him, hoping to marry him, to continue our business connections, our family ties."

"I see." The two words fell flatly between them, but Serena didn't see at all! Such things were strange to her English way of thinking. But she supposed such a marriage could work, couldn't it? Maria was young, pretty and pliable. Roberto would mould her to his ways and they would make a suitably handsome couple.

So why did her heart ache, her thoughts resent it? It was nothing to do with her, none of her business. There was nothing she could do now to make up to Maria for Gino's defection. But she did understand now why the young girl was so unfriendly towards her. Did she begrudge too the time Roberto spent with her and Nicky?

Unconsciously, she gave a deep sigh.

"Try to forget it, Serena *cara*. You and the little one are becoming dear to us, *si*?"

Just then Nicky came bursting in with his grandfather following.

"Nonno is going to show me how to whistle, Mum." For ages he'd been trying to master the art, without success, for neither his mother nor Lettie could help him.

"In that case, I'll leave you," his *nonna* laughed, and Serena helped her to gather up her sewing and go indoors.

Roberto was just coming out of his

study with an armful of folders and a briefcase.

"Ah, Serena — I can't stop, I'm away up to the vineyard to see if things are ready for our move. I wondered — would you let me take you to dinner when I get back tonight? Perhaps outdoors, beside the lake?"

Caught unawares, she stammered, "Oh, I've promised to take Nicky one night. You've just reminded me. I'm sorry, Roberto, but I did promise — just the two of us . . . " Somehow she felt cross with herself for having to refuse him. But moonlit dinners just weren't on were they? Not for her and Roberto. And she didn't know what made her suggest, "Why not take Maria? I'm sure she'd love to go."

A flash of anger showed for a second in his dark eyes. He shook his head, turning to go. "Some other time maybe. *Ciao*."

So it was that when siesta time came round she persuaded Nicky to have a rest on his bed.

"Will I stay up late?" His face shone with delight at this grown-up concession.

"Very late, pet. That's why we're having a rest this afternoon."

"Will it be dark? Are we dressing up?"

"Very dark, but there's strings of lights everywhere. And yes, love, it's best clothes tonight."

She lowered the slatted blinds and left him, still trying to whistle through his baby teeth!

He was bubbling over with excitement as they dressed that night. And he looked a real little man in his dark trousers and white silk shirt finished off by the small velvet bow tie.

Serena had done him proud too. Her dark grey silk shift with its shoelace shoulder straps was lightened by the blue stones in the filigree silver necklace, and matching bracelet. Her lovely fair hair was pleated on the nape of her slender neck, her blue/green eyes emphasized by subtle eyeshadow.

Watching over her shoulder as she finished her make-up, her son's face shone with pride. And Serena was determined that tonight he would feel like her grown-up escort!

It was a beautiful evening, warm enough to dispense with a wrap. The cobalt-blue lake reflected the rows of coloured lights, the flickering candles. All along the bank of the lake, the tables and chairs, a different colour for each restaurant, were laid out ready. Sure-footed waiters in black and white hurried swiftly down the aisles, musicians played the old Italian lovesongs. And everywhere there was an air of festivity, of romance.

For a sad, brief moment she longed to be part of that romantic scene, and then she chided herself for the stupid longing.

They were able to park her car on the main street, and with solemn decorum Nicky placed his small hand on her arm and guided her through the parading throng.

With some inherent instinct, he chose the best restaurant and helped his mother into a seat right on the waters edge. From a rowing boat in the middle of the lake full of youngsters came the sound of an accordion completing the enchanting setting.

"Signora signor." With a flourish, their waiter passed them each a long elaborate menu and she waited patiently while Nicky made his choice. Used to Italian food, he chose wisely and her heart swelled with pride. One day, when she was an old woman, she would remember this night, she told herself sentimentally.

A group of local *ragazzi* passed by as they were eating shouting out envious remarks, but Nicky just ignored them. And again she was pleased with him. There were times when she wondered if she and Lettie were bringing him up well, but tonight wasn't one of them!

He was allowed a little red wine

watered down, and he sipped from the slender stemmed glass as if it held pure nectar.

It was much later as they were drinking their coffee, that a dark figure suddenly slipped into the spare seat at their table.

"Zio! It's Uncle Roberto."

"*Ciao* Nico. Hello Serena, I hope you don't mind? I thought I'd come to take you home."

Swallowing hard against the pounding of her heart, she replied quietly, "Thanks Roberto, but there was no need. My car's over there."

"Yes, I saw it — that's how I found you both. I've sent my car back, so we can all take yours."

A quick protest rose to her lips and then, for Nicky's sake, she held it back. Was he being high-handed, or was it just another example of Latin protectiveness?

"Come along then son, we might as well go." Her tone let him know how much she resented his intrusion into what had been Nicky's night out with his mother.

"Would you rather take a walk first?"

"No, it's getting late and Nicky's tired," she replied coldly.

"I'm not, Mum!" Nicky protested struggling to open tired eyes wider. Stiff-backed, she walked across to her car and dropped the keys into Roberto's outstretched hand. Tired or not, Nicky snuggled down on the back seat and was asleep almost before they reached the road to Bardolino.

"You didn't take Maria out then?" she broke the silence, her voice cool.

"I can choose my own partners, Serena."

Again the silence hung like a curtain between them until she informed him, "Nonna told me this morning — about Maria and Gino."

"Pity!" he answered tersely. "You've suffered enough at his hands, I wish you hadn't had to find out. But, of course, we didn't know he was already married."

"Don't worry, Roberto, the time has long passed when Gino's exploits bothered me."

He drove slowly, the headlights picking out the beauty of the night, the trees rushing past, the scurry of the little night creatures.

"Am I forgiven, *cara*, for the awful things I said to you, the way I acted that time in London?"

She moved restlessly in her seat, and then swallowing hard told him, "You didn't know me then. I've forgotten it."

"Good." Again came a long pause, and then he said softly, "You look lovely tonight, Serena. Nicky was so proud of you, I could tell."

"And I of him," she put in as he went on, "That necklace matched your eyes — and the bracelet."

She felt a sudden irritation — what was he up to now? Funny though that the irritation should give her that odd, hurting tug at her heartstrings.

"Gino gave me the bracelet for my

eighteenth birthday, just before we were married. I bought the necklace to match later."

"You still wear the bracelet . . . " There was a question in his voice.

"Yes," she replied scathingly, "it reminds me of how nàive I was — a silly, romantic little fool. Reminds me never to be taken in by a man again."

"As I told you before, all Ercoli men are not as Gino was. Please believe me." There was a gentle pleading in the words that she didn't want to hear.

She shrugged, glad to see that they had reached the Casa d'Ercoli. He opened the door for her, handing her out of the car, but instead of letting go of her hand, he raised it to his lips.

"Goodnight, *cara*, sleep well." And with that, he turned and carried the sleeping youngster up to his bedroom.

And for a long time after getting into bed, Serena felt the touch of his lips on her hand. She ought to keep away from him. There was danger from the expression in that man's dark eyes, his attractive looks. Danger to her own foolish heart that quickened too often when he was near.

Was there danger, too, to Nicky?

★ ★ ★

"I'm bored, Mum," Nicky complained and Serena sympathized with him. She felt rather at a loose end herself, and he was missing the attention of his grandparents. Maria Donati had gone back that morning to her home and the two Ercolis had decided to go with her to see their old friends and neighbours before the move up to the vineyard.

"Why don't you go and feed the tortoise, love. Get him some lettuce from the kitchen," she suggested. "Perhaps the cook's children will go with you too."

As Nicky scampered off gleefully kitchenwards, he collided with his uncle just coming into the lounge.

"Why the haste, Serena?" He smiled

fondly after the small figure of his nephew.

And as Serena explained, she added, "I'm a bit restless myself, Roberto. Guess I'm so used to working . . . "

"Have you been to Verona yet?" he asked.

She shook her head. "Not yet — why?"

"Come with me. I can spare this morning." His voice was casual, carefully hiding the anticipation he felt. He so rarely got her alone! "Leave Nicky to play in the garden. I'll get one of the maids to watch out for him, si?"

"No!" she burst out, and then, seeing the look on his face, she went on hurriedly, "I mean no I don't want to leave Nicky, but yes I'd love to go to Verona with you."

He hid his disappointment with a smile.

"Good. I'll get the car and see you in about ten minutes."

But Nicky had found his playmates and very definitely didn't want 'to go and see some more old places'. But Serena insisted, so they did not start out in the best of moods. But after refusing Roberto's invitation to dine out with him, she felt they should make an effort to enjoy the trip to Verona. Besides, she felt safer all round with him with her.

The ancient town was crowded with holiday-makers, and Nicky soon became annoyed at being pushed and jostled. Parking the car had been difficult . . . and then it started to rain! And when it rains in Verona it really pours down. They dodged umbrellas and splashes from old guttering. Even the famous Romeo and Juliet balcony looked rather unromantic and wet, and Nicky began to drag his feet in disgust.

The only thing that amused him was the sight of a very large German trying to struggle into one of the cheap, skimpy plastic macs being sold by the score by a street vendor. It only fitted halfway round.

"He ought to buy two, Mum," Nicky giggled, much to Serena's dismay.

Roberto caught her arm and guided them all into the nearest café. "It's no good, *cara*. We'll have a coffee and then go home." The place was crowded; steaming with heat and wet clothes. The coffee was as good as ever though.

Serena felt rather sorry for Roberto. His treat was turning out to be a wash-out in every way! When he paid their bill at the little cash desk he brought Nicky a packet of sweets. Once in the car, he turned to Serena and with a large clean white hankie reached out to wipe the raindrops from her face.

"Mi dispiace, cara." His voice was soft, and the touch of his hand sent a tremor through her veins. When Roberto was being kind and gentle, he could make her heart beat like a drum!

"You can't help the weather — don't worry. A drop of rain never hurt anybody." Just then he moved his head sending a shower of wet from his hair on to her face, wetting it again.

At that, they both began to laugh — just as the sun came out again.

★ ★ ★

The next morning, he was just finishing his rolls and coffee when she went into the small breakfast-room.

"Good morning, Serena. *Come sta?*"

"Very well, Roberto, *grazie.*"

"Before I go, I was wondering if you'd like Nico to learn to ride?" He paused to put conserve on his roll and butter. "There is a small stable quite near with a suitable little pony and a good tutor." He watched her face closely as if trying to judge her reaction. A sudden chill swept over her as she sensed yet another danger to her son. "I assure you he will be quite safe. He would probably like it."

Of course he would, she knew that, so what could she do but accept?

250

"Of course. Thank you, Roberto, for the offer."

"Good, I will fix it today and you can take him."

Nicky was highly delighted, though not too keen on the hard hat the tutor insisted on his wearing. Taking him in the car, determined to make sure of his safety, she liked the middle-aged owner on sight. He chatted to Nicky in a mixture of Italian and English — not talking down to him, but leaving no doubt about his authority. The small pony obviously adored him and stood quietly patient under Nicky's tentative touch.

Seated on a bale of hay, Serena watched the bowlegged Bruno guide the pony round and round the small yard on a leading rein, a thrilled Nicky looking as if he'd been riding for ages.

"Faster, Bruno, *avanti*," he urged excitedly. To her relief, she saw the man shake his head.

"Presto, piccino, presto." And he

lifted the boy down far too soon for his liking.

"*Domani, si?*"

"Yes please. *Grazie*, Bruno."

"*Prego*, Nico, *domani*."

And that night at dinner, he couldn't wait to tell his grandparents all about his first riding lesson.

"Bruno says he has the making of a good horseman, Serena," Roberto told her confidentially. So he had already spoken to the stable owner, had he?

In spite of her suspicions, his concern touched her; did he really care for his nephew? In a softer mood, she let him walk her into the garden after dinner.

"Thank you for arranging the riding lessons for Nicky. He really loved it this morning," she smiled, remembering the picture of her young son sitting up so proudly on the little chestnut-coloured pony. "He'll be up at crack of dawn tomorrow, I expect."

"*Bene*, I'm glad I pleased you, *cara*." His voice was husky. She was terribly conscious of the undercurrents, the fine thread of tension and mutual longing vibrating between them in the warmth of the night. Desperately her mind cast around for something to say, to break the spell.

"Why haven't you married, Roberto?" Even as she spoke, she knew she had said the wrong thing. She stole a quick, surreptitious glance at him, but the look on his tanned face was unreadable, enigmatic. In the long pause, she could almost hear the deep thud of her own heart.

"*I* didn't want an arranged marriage, Serena. I want to choose my own partner; didn't want a typical obedient little Italian wife."

She recalled then that he had used the word partner before.

"I wanted someone who loved me, myself, not as the eldest Ercoli heir; not as a marriage bargain. But someone to be the other half of me."

His voice was low, almost as if he had forgotten she was there. She swallowed hard against the lump in her throat, hoping he wouldn't regret his confidences in the morning.

"So there, Serena, you know now why I'm still a *solo* — unmarried. Of course, there have been the little 'loves'," — she saw him shrug as he continued — "but up till now well, I still seek my other half."

"*Capisco*. I hope you find her, Roberto, soon." Again he gave that so Latin shrug, and she truly hoped that he would find happiness, that his marriage would not be the empty mockery his younger brother's had been.

★ ★ ★

The weeks flashed by. Every morning Nicky had his riding lesson, and in the afternoon, he played with the servants' assorted bunch of children.

At the weekend, Roberto finally announced that it was time to move up to the vineyard and for the next two days all was chaos. Excited, garrulous voices made it sound as if World

War III had broken out!

Poor Nicky was torn between his longing to go and his unwillingness to leave the little pony behind.

"Don't worry, Nico, there are many horses up there. Take your hard hat." Busy as he was, Roberto spared time for his nephew. "A big shady one too."

Many of the staff were going with them and the luggage was to be taken by truck the day before. Dust covers were thrown over the beautiful old furniture; shutters closed against the sun, and all was to be left in the charge of one or two older servants.

When the time came to go, Serena was sorry to say goodbye to the Casa d'Ercoli, especially the lovely gardens with their view of the blue lake. Would she see it again, she wondered.

It was a pleasant journey, climbing up steadily to the well-wooded area high above Verona. Clumps of grey gnarled olive trees stood like crooked sentinels, as they had done for hundreds of years.

She wished she could have driven more slowly and enjoyed the scenery, but she had difficulty in keeping her eye on Roberto's big car ahead. At last they saw the beginning of the growing vines; slope after slope; rows and rows as far as the eye could see, straight lines of thick green leaves.

"Look, Mum, they look just like rows of soldiers. Look how straight they are." Excitedly Nicky hung out of the car window, trying to see everything at once. Until at last they drew near the vineyard. Driving past huge sheds, with lorries and carts and every kind of equipment standing there, waiting for the day when all those bright green rows would be laden with luscious grapes ready to harvest.

It looked all so factory-like and her heart sank. After the beauty of Lake Garda, this all seemed so . . . drab. That is until they came to the old villa standing back and high above the big building. The stucco walls had been newly pink-washed, the old verandah, which ran three sides of it, was grey with lichen and age. As were the slatted shutters that kept out the fierceness of the sun.

But up there, the air was cooler, fresher, with the wonderful aroma of growing vines.

"Come, little one," his *nonna* took Nicky's arm and led him indoors. After the bright sunlight it seemed dim inside, but the rooms were big and airy. Polished wood floors were lightened by colourful rugs; and heavy old furniture plain and simple and useful.

Again Nicky was given a small room off his mother's, and they were to share a bathroom with Roberto and Lucia. Noise was everywhere, indoors with the unpacking, shouted instructions. Outdoors was the sound of engines and dogs barking.

"Guard dogs," Roberto told her. "Don't worry, during the day they are in a keeper's care."

"Can I go and look round, Zio?" Nicky couldn't wait to explore.

"*Certamente*, but keep near to the villa for now, Nico."

Seeing the flash of anxiety on Serena's face, he hastened to assure her, "Don't worry, there are many workers out there to watch him."

"What are they — we doing up here? The grapes are not formed yet?"

"Not even the flowers that come first in June, *cara*. But right now, there is lots to do. All the vines must be tied up, trained along the fences, ready to take the weight of the bunches of grapes. Also they must all be checked carefully for phylloxera — a kind of mildew that is often found in the root stock. Just pray we have no rain until the flowers are set. Besides, we find it cooler up here, no tourists, more private."

"I see. Can we help?" she asked.

"Of course. Every pair of hands is needed in the tying up, *cara*." As they stood there talking, there was suddenly a harsh scream, the fearsome growls of a dog — savage and wild.

Petrified, Serena screamed, "Nicky!" Then she turned and fled outdoors, frantic eyes looking around, her legs weak and trembling, her heart lurching with fear. Then she heard Nicky's terrified cries coming from behind a clump of trees, and she started to run towards it. But Roberto passed her, shouting loudly to the dog, calling for help.

Never would she forget the sight that met her anguished eyes! Nicky's body was beneath a huge dog, his clothes torn, blood on his hands, his eyes glazed with terror. By the time Roberto had pulled the dog away, several workers had also reached the scene. Picking up the sobbing boy, he hurried back to the house, his face livid with anger, calling out threats to the man who had let this happen.

"Madre, ring for the doctor." He laid the sobbing boy on the settee, demanding hot water, bandages. With shaking hands, Serena helped him to strip off the shredded clothes, trying to gently soothe her son.

By the time the elderly doctor arrived, Nicky's wounds had been bathed and his sobs were subsiding. In rapid Italian Roberto explained what had happened and the doctor gave him an injection, while his uncle held his hand, murmuring words of comfort.

"You are the brave one, Nico, rest easy."

Once the little boy was asleep, Roberto stormed out, determined to see who was responsible for the dog being loose. Half an hour later, he returned to tell Serena, "He says the dog was on its chain . . . "

"How could it have been?" she stormed, still suffering from the shock.

"I believe him; he has been with us for years and would not lie to me." Roberto was adamant, but she still shook her head in disbelief. "Trust me, *cara*, I will get to the bottom of this. I am sending the dog away to another part of the estate. I will take Nico round later with me to introduce him to the other guard dogs. Don't worry *cara* he will be all right once they know him."

She turned away, her heart like lead. Was this yet another attempt on her son's life? But Roberto had been with her and Lucia had not yet arrived. So — who could have done this? Or was it just an accident? Dear God! If only she knew . . .

Fortunately, Nicky's injuries were slight, but he had been badly frightened. He had thought the dog friendly and had approached it to stroke it.

"Serena, he'll be fine. All little boys have a tangle with a dog at some time, *cara*."

The look of despair on her face made him reach out to pull her close. Gently he smoothed back the curtain of silken blonde hair, and the touch of his hands sent a quiver through her body. How could she be so moved by this man's nearness when he could have been the one who brought about her son's injury?

The warmth of his lips on her hair made her nerves tingle and left her heart racing like mad.

"Oh Roberto . . . " With a heartfelt little sigh, she moved out of his arms, wishing she didn't long to respond to his kiss.

How could she? Self-disgust made her feel angry with herself. She went to see that Nicky was still sleeping and then strolled out on to the verandah, staring moist-eyed at the scenery. As she did something moved in the shadow of the flower-laden bushes. She caught her breath; it was the tall thin man — that man who had appeared everywhere she'd been since they came to Italy! One glimpse, and then he was gone. Could she have been mistaken; there were so many men working here?

Her head throbbed, and she felt as if she was going mad. With no proof, how could she be sure that all these incidents were not accidental? As Roberto had said — many kids patted the wrong dog.

As they drank their coffee after dinner that night, she turned to him and asked casually, "I keep seeing a man — a tall, thin man — everywhere we go. Is he one of your staff?" Seeing his surprise at the question, she gave a little laugh. "All Italians look very much alike to me, but it does seem funny. He's always there."

He could tell that this was something that was really bothering her.

"Point him out to me, *cara*, next time, *si*?" She nodded, not wanting to tell him how often the man had quickly vanished, only to appear again somewhere else. "When we have settled in, I'll take you and Nico round the vineyards. Do you ride? Maybe on horseback would be pleasant, *si*?"

"Let me get used to a horse again first, Roberto. Nicky too. There aren't many chances of horse riding in Central London, you know."

"I'll tell my stable boy to come and see you, *cara*." He reached out and placed his lean hand over hers as it

263

rested beside her coffee cup. "I hope you like it up here, Serena — that you and I can get to know one another better. Nico, too."

Sudden heat rose in her at his touch; every vibrant nerve in her body ached to respond. Angry at the longing that was making her heart beat so erratically, she withdrew her hand from beneath his. And even as she did, she sensed his dismay, so she picked up a spoon and began to stir her already cold coffee.

Later Lucia hurried in, making voluble apologies to her parents in rapid Italian for her delay.

"*Non si preoccupi*, Lucia *cara*. Sit, sit down and eat," her mother begged her and ordered the maid to bring in some food for the late-comer. Lucia took a seat, and reaching out for some wine, paused to look scornfully across at Serena.

"So! You are still here. I thought you would have returned to England. Surely Nico needs to be back at school by now?"

"Quiet, Lucia," her father snapped sternly. "*Lei si shaglia* — you're wrong, *figlia*. We want Serena and Nico up here with us." And the look he gave his daughter clearly showed his marked displeasure at the remarks.

"You'll spoil the boy and he will miss his lessons." The spite was still there on Lucia's face.

"It's good of you to be so concerned, Lucia," Serena answered calmly, "but I've brought his school books, and Nicky will soon be having some lessons with me up here, don't worry."

"I think the little one is learning all the time," put in her father-in-law. "His Italian improves, and so does my English." He smiled fondly. "He will get to know about the vineyards, our wines, the countryside. There is much to learn outside of the books."

"When we have been here a little longer, I want to give a party," his wife told them. "To let our old friends up here meet our grandson and his mother."

The old man nodded his approval, but Serena could tell that Lucia was far from pleased. With an angry snap of her teeth, she pushed away her plate, the food unfinished.

"I'll go and unpack. And leave you to your plans," she said bitterly. Good manners made the older couple refrain from comment on their daughter's rude behaviour, but it was obvious that they were annoyed with her.

Early the following morning, Serena found herself gently trotting beside her young son. True to his word, Roberto had told his stable hand to choose suitable mounts for them both.

The stable boy — all of fifty-odd years — with a face like a wrinkled walnut, was delighted to show them around the stables. The smell of horses, leather and sweat was pungent, but she could see that the animals were obviously in good condition, well cared for.

"Me, I am Milo, *signora*, and this — " he patted a beautiful mare fondly — "this is La Contessa. Is she not *bella*?"

Indeed she was; a lovely light chestnut with a long silky mane and tail, she trotted with a delicately proud air as befitted her name. Serena adored her on sight, telling herself to be always careful of her gentle mouth. A suitable small pony was chosen for Nicky.

"Just like my mother," he said delightedly. "*Grazie*, Milo."

Beaming, Milo led his charges out of the cobbled yard towards the shady path.

For a couple of hours each morning they rode with Milo along the bridle paths up and down the hills. In the afternoons, Nicky had simple lessons with his mother in his room, or with his *nonno*.

It pleased her to see how intensely he listened to the old man, each laughingly correcting the other's language mistakes. She could see how fond he was becoming of his grandparents; Roberto too. There was a hint of hero-worship in the growing attachment to his uncle, and she wondered how he would react to going back to London when the time came.

★ ★ ★

"Show me round the sheds, Roberto," she begged one day when he didn't seem too busy. She had offered to help with the tying up of the growing vines, but he always put her off. It was back-breaking work, and he didn't want her to do it.

"After lunch then, *cara*. Flat shoes," he reminded her with a smile.

"Can I come too, Zio?" Nicky asked eagerly.

"If you promise to be careful, Nico."

The first thing that struck them both was the size of the buildings. They stretched up so high too; almost out of sight.

"So big," she breathed, "and so cool and dark."

"Italy is the biggest wine producing

country in the world." There was a wealth of pride in Roberto's voice. He showed them the fermenting vats, the hydraulic presses, the crushing and destalking machines. Huge wine casks, each standing taller than a man, ranged in rows, with iron stairs here and there leading above to a wide platform where still more casks stood, as they had for so many years.

"I thought they'd all be empty until later," she said pensively. At that he began to tell her of the various blending processes still going on there.

"We produce a good Valpolicella, the light red. The white Soave, and of course, the well-known Bardolino. We still produce a little Chianti, just for our own consumption," he went on, pleased at her interest. Nicky was taking all this in, wide-eyed and keen to see everything, especially the huge oak casks stored in the old sheds that had their back walls carved out of the hillside like caves.

Here and there they stopped to

sample various wines, drawn off by the big glass syphons.

"Try this, *cara*. Is it not *amabile* — soft to the mouth?" In fact the medium sweet red wine was indeed gentle to the palate, soft and fruity.

"I'll be tipsy," she smiled up at him, her greeny/blue eyes wide above the rim of the old crystal wine glass.

Out in the fresh air again, she did feel somewhat light-headed, but it was so good to be back amongst the wine trade she loved so well.

"Where are we going now, Zio?" Nicky couldn't wait to see everything and was skipping ahead and back again, urging them on.

"These are the bottling sheds; the labelling and packing department." Long benches, stacks of flattened cardboard cartons, piles of highly coloured labels. And here and there the jars and siphons, the meters, for testing the strength and sweetness of each wine. Round the edge of this vast hall were other smaller rooms.

"Locked, I'm afraid — full of our secrets."

"Let me see," Nicky begged, but Roberto shook his head, ruffling his nephew's dark head with a fond hand.

"Locked up. Here you can have these," and he handed over a bunch of the beautiful multi-coloured and gold-edged labels he had collected as they went round.

Highly pleased, Nicky told him, "I'll put these on my bedroom wall." But he finally got bored as the two grown-ups still stood chatting about wines and yet more wines.

She takes more interest than Lucia does — or Gino ever did, Roberto mused, watching her lovely cool face, the silver gleams in the silken hair. Her fairness enchanted him, and he felt he could never see enough of it. His silence made her glance up through long thick lashes, and as she saw the look in his eyes, she felt a sudden flood of desire spread through her limbs with a bone-melting weakness that set her

271

heart throbbing madly.

She swallowed against the constriction in her throat.

"I must catch up with Nicky . . . " To her disgust, her voice was thick and husky. The heat scorched her cheeks as she turned and hurried after her son, leaving the tall dark man watching her flight with a look of longing on his face.

8

"**I** AM still trying to find your mystery man, Serena," Roberto told her at breakfast a few days later.

"And . . . ?" she turned to him eagerly, only to see him shake his head.

"No luck, not really. Odd men have said they think they have seen him, but that it could have been a local. Another thought he had brought one of the trucks up from the *Casa* and then gone back down again. So . . . " He spread his hand wide, "But don't worry, *cara*, I will keep a lookout, so will my men. If he's prowling around here, we will get him."

"*Grazie*, Roberto, I hope you do. There's something about the thought of him that scares me."

Putting down his napkin, he rose to leave for work.

"How about a ride to see the vines after lunch, Serena?"

"Nicky too? I don't want to leave him." If he was disappointed at not being able to get her alone, he hid it well.

"Of course, *cara*." He smiled down at her. "*Ciao* for now then." There was something about that smile that lifted her heart and she looked forward to their ride later.

★ ★ ★

In their hard hats; with a light sweater over their cotton shirts and with slim-fitting denim trousers, they joined him at the stables after a light lunch. It had been difficult to get the over-eager Nicky to sit down for lunch at all!

With Roberto in the lead on a tall frisky black stallion, Nicky followed, with Serena in the rear. For once she felt safe. Roberto knew the way, and Nicky was well within her sight. As they set out, the path was fairly narrow, rough and tree-lined. The air was clear, the sky above bright blue and cloudless, and Roberto's instructions came back to them distinctly.

"Not far now, Nico," he replied as Nicky asked yet again how much further.

Then, without warning, for one heart-stopping moment, terror tore at her throat as an arm was thrust out from the bushes. An arm uplifted, wielding a thick wooden branch. One swift blow descended with a hard crack on the rump of Nicky's small pony.

Serena screamed a warning as the frightened little animal reared up and then bolted.

"Roberto! Oh my God — Nicky!" The pony had brushed past the tall stallion, to gallop off, wide-eyed with terror, with Nicky clinging desperately to its mane. Even as Serena screamed out, Roberto had calmed his unnerved beast and set off in pursuit. Calling out, soothing the pony in soft Italian, he pulled on its reins, carefully slowing it down in a cloud of dust.

But his own mettlesome mount chose that very moment to show his own anger and reared up, catching Roberto off guard. And, as the horse rose on its back legs, Roberto's head struck a heavy branch above, almost unseating him.

Frantically, Serena urged her horse alongside him, trying to catch him, support him. She never knew just what happened next. Somehow she threw herself from the saddle, just in time to break the fall to the ground of Roberto's inert body.

"Oh God, he's dead . . . " Kneeling beside him on the rough ground, she cradled his dark head in her lap. Already there was the sign of an ugly swelling and a badly torn wound on his forehead. His face had a deathly pallor, his eyes closed tightly, his breathing shallow. "Dear heavens, don't let him die . . . "

And in that moment, that hour-long moment, she knew . . . knew that if anything happened to this man, she wanted to die too.

What could she do? As her arms held him close to her breast, she felt absolutely helpless.

Nicky, with great courage for so young a child, had reached the black horse, and murmuring soothingly, had managed to tie its reins to a tree further down the path. Gingerly he turned his pony and trotted back to them, staring down at his uncle, his lips trembling, big tears streaming down his cheeks.

"Mum, is he . . . ? Oh Mum, look, he's bleeding."

For once, Serena hardly took in what her son was saying. All her concern, all her love just then was for the man whose blood was seeping away.

"Nicky, go . . . " she began and then drew in a sharp breath. "No, you can't go alone." What could she do? She couldn't risk sending Nicky back for help — not with a dangerous assailant still lurking about! She would have to go, take the boy with her . . . and leave Roberto alone. Still in danger?

"Dear heavens," her hands shook, her legs felt as if they'd never support her.

"Give me your sweater, Nicky." She peeled off her own and put the two of them beneath Roberto's head as she lowered it gently to the ground. Tenderly, she placed a soft kiss on the uninjured cheek.

"I'll be back soon, my darling." She struggled up into the saddle and turned her horse. "Come on, Nicky — carefully."

She longed to break into a fast gallop, but knew her son could only manage a canter. Every inch of the way seemed endless. Her heart felt as if it would break with anguish for the beloved man she'd had to leave there behind.

As they finally rode into the stable yard, she yelled out, calling for help, telling Nicky to go and tell his grandparents, to stay with them . . .

Frantically she urged the men to bring a jeep. Clambering into the back, she again gave them directions as they drove rapidly along the path.

He hadn't moved. The blood had clotted on his face and his white shirt. His breathing was not quite so bad, but his eyes were still tightly closed, a waxy pallor round his mouth.

The men lifted him gently on to the smelly horse-blanket, resting his head in Serena's lap. She tucked the sweaters round his shoulders holding him close against the sway of the Jeep's speed.

Over and over, a prayer on her lips, she begged him to open his eyes, to speak to her. In the depth of her despair she blamed herself.

"I shouldn't have come to Italy. Oh Roberto, my love . . . " and the bitter tears flowed down her cheeks, on to his.

His parents, faces grey with anxiety, met them in the drive.

"Is he . . . ?" Oriana Ercoli almost collapsed when she looked at her son lying there.

"He's all right, Nonna. He'll be all right."

"*Il dottore* — the doctor is coming." There was a blue edge to the old man's pale lips, but he gave calm instructions to the men; helped to get his son on to the bed and into a clean shirt. And still Roberto gave no sign of returning consciousness.

After his examination, the grey-haired doctor told them that Roberto was badly concussed, and that there was nothing to be done, except to wait until he came round.

"I doubt I can get a nurse in today. In any case, he will probably surface in a few hours. Don't worry, *signora*, he is young and strong."

His words were little comfort to Serena or his mother, who told the doctor, "We will watch over him all the time."

"We'll take turns, Nonna. I'll stay the night; I'm younger. You and Nonno stay till then, *si*?"

"Bless you, *nuora*."

They watched the doctor's departure, and above them, Lucia was standing looking down at her brother, her usually austere face contorted with grief and shock.

"Oh no, Roberto, it was not meant for you," she whispered brokenly.

★ ★ ★

Later that night, after seeing her son to bed, Serena made arrangements to stay the night watching over the still unconscious man. There was an old-fashioned *chaise-longue* in his room, and with pillows and a rug, she was able to rest. She turned off all but one small bedside lamp and, wrapped in a cool cotton housecoat, she lay quietly, her thoughts giving her no peace.

This time, there was no doubt at all — someone had definitely tried to injure Nicky. Once more she saw that awful moment in her mind's eye. Yes, it had been a man's arm she had seen.

281

In the morning, she would ring for the police; tell them all that had happened. Her father-in-law had insisted that men should be posted round the villa as well as one on the landing outside the bedroom. At least Nicky would be safe tonight, she told herself.

Just then she heard a sound — Roberto was stirring! Leaning over him, she saw his head tossing from side to side, words tumbling from his dry lips.

"Roberto, open your eyes, *caro* please," she begged, hot tears stinging behind her eyelids.

"Serena? *Cristo mio*! What happened?" His hand reached up to feel the lump on his forehead, now swollen and multi-coloured.

"Hush, *caro*. You are all right now, rest easy."

"What happened? Nicky — is he safe?" He struggled to focus his eyes on her face and then touched her wet cheek. "*Lacrima? Non piange, cara.* Don't cry."

"Oh, my dearest, I thought you were dead — your poor head." She swallowed against her tears, smoothing a lock of the dark hair gently away from his face. "Nicky is fine, he's asleep in his bed, don't worry."

"I remember now, his pony bolted."

"You hit your head on a branch and you've been unconscious since then," she told him quietly.

"I'm thirsty."

Lifting his head, she gave him a drink from the vacuum flask beside the bed. He sighed deeply, looking better every second.

"What time is it?" he asked.

"Two o'clock — in the morning."

"Then what are you doing here?" With a struggle, he raised himself on the pillows.

"Waiting for you to come round." She reached out and clasped his hand. "You gave us such a fright, *Fratello*, you looked dreadful."

"Well, I feel all right now except for a thick head," he paused, watching her

283

closely. "Seem to remember someone begging me not to die — somebody's tears splashing down on my face." His eyes held such a wealth of tenderness that her heart began to pound, her breath tight in her throat. He indicated the bed beside him.

"Come here, Serena, closer." The words were low and husky.

Drawing the thin housecoat round her slim waist, she lay down beside him, hoping he would not hear the thudding of her heart, her every vibrant nerve in her body aware of his nearness.

"*Veramente*? Is it true — did I hear that?" Long lashes covered her eyes as she nodded, not daring to trust her voice. "Serena, *bellissima*, I've wanted to do this for so long . . . "

He reached out and turned her towards him. She could feel his touch scorching through the thin material at her back, and his hands pressed her even closer, ever closer, body moulding to body. And then his dark head blotted out the light as his lips found hers.

Gently, softly at first, and then as his passion rose, the kiss deepened, drawing every breath from her body. And in that first long kiss it seemed that she awakened to life as surely as any sleeping beauty.

"Oh, Serena, *amore*. *Voglio* — I want you so much." Incoherently his words in jumbled Italian and English spilled out, filling her with happiness she'd never known. Roberto who could turn her body to limpid acquiescence with his touch, his kiss, wanted her . . . "*Mia adorata*. I love you, *cara*. I think I loved you from the first moment we met. But how could I tell you — ask you to love me — another Ercoli man?"

"I know now, darling, you are nothing like Gino." As she spoke, his lips were kissing her cheeks, her eyes, travelling down the erotic curve of her neck. Desire tingled along her skin, leaving her heart racing, her breathing shallow.

It had been so long since she'd been

loved. Her body ached with need; cried out to be touched, aroused. Slowly he moved aside her wrap, and as he nuzzled the soft swell of her breasts, she felt her nipples grow taut, pulsating with passionate abandon. He stroked first one proud peak and then the other with an indolent thumb, dark eyes beneath darker lashes watching her face as she moved voluptuously against him.

Luxuriating in his lovemaking, she felt her flesh tingle against the matt of black hairs on his chest that arrowed down to his navel. He felt warm and firm beneath her exploring fingers. And as she touched him, he drew in a deep breath, murmuring hoarsely against her lips. As her soft body moulded itself against his, desire, hot and heady made her long to lose herself in passionate surrender.

She couldn't remember ever experiencing anything quite so sensual as the deliberate way his hands moved over her sensitized skin. Daringly, she let her own hands wander — touching, exploring, lower and lower. And as she did, she felt his manhood harden against her thigh and knew that her need for him was something basic and all-consuming.

With a swift movement he laid her over on to her back, discarding the garments that came between them. His kisses were tormenting her as he explored the corners of her mouth, bit her soft bottom lip, and all the time his wandering fingers sought the hidden core of her femininity.

"Please, *cara*," he begged, in a voice hoarse with desire that matched her own. Her head moved from side to side — wanting him — wanting to feel him inside her.

"Yes, oh yes, Roberto, now . . . "

There was a tiny hint of pain, and then she felt the length of him, filling her, making her complete. Gently at first and then with an ever-increasing pounding, he thrust deeper and deeper, and she wrapped her slim legs tightly around his buttocks, holding him ever closer.

Sweat beaded his brow, her top lip. Sanity was abandoned in a chaotic whirl of red-hot passion as she opened herself to him, holding him tightly with her thighs. Harder and harder they moved together, heat pounding thrust after thrust. And then she climaxed — high above the clouds, among the stars. An explosion she'd never known before. For a wonderful moment she hung there, high in ecstasy. And then she fell — down to earth, to lie panting as Roberto watched her, tender triumph gleaming in his dark eyes.

"Bene?" Gasping, she nodded and then felt him begin the age-old ritual again. Until at last, with an animal-like groan, he collapsed on top of her. And she felt his hot seed spill into her as she lay, languorously satiated — a woman at last! "Now we are one, my love," he whispered softly in her ear. "You are my other half." And he kissed her to sleep in his arms as the dawn gradually

sent its fingers of light over the sleeping couple lying, limbs entwined, on the big old bed.

Before it was fully light, Roberto eased himself out of bed, his head still throbbing as he moved. And tenderly, he lifted the sleeping girl and gently placed her on the *chaise-longue*, watching her for a moment before covering her with the blanket.

The doctor came in to see him soon after breakfast, and peering into his bloodshot eyes, told him to stay in bed for the rest of the day.

"Buon giorno, cara." Surrounded by papers he sat propped against a bank of pillows when Serena went in to see him. His face lit up with pleasure whilst hers flushed as she remembered what had happened on that big bed a few hours before!

He held out his hands, a wicked glitter in his uninjured eye. With a soft cry, she flew across the room into his outstretched arms.

"How are you this morning, darling?"

"The happiest man in all of Italy, *cara*," he murmured against her willing lips. "No — in all the world!"

And for a little while the rest of that world fell away and there was only the two of them in it.

"Say nothing about us to the family, Serena, until we have had time to talk," he told her. "There is something I must see about this morning." All the same, he was reluctant to let her go.

Downstairs, she found her mother-in-law in the conservatory.

"*Ciao*, Serena, *cara*. You look well this morning." Serena's face was radiant with happiness; she looked so obviously like a woman in love, beloved.

An almost shy look in her blue eyes, she smiled back at Nonna.

"I feel fine — and you?" The old lady nodded, hoping her suspicions were correct.

"I am just making some notes for the party. I think Saturday night will do, and I want you to help me, *si*?"

"Of course. Let me see what Nicky's

doing first, will you?"

Upstairs, Lucia had taken in the post to Roberto and was waiting for his instructions about the day's business.

"Sit down, Lucia, I want to speak with you."

A frightened, wary looked shadowed her face then. She clasped her hands tightly in her lap as Roberto went on, "You said 'not for me' didn't you? Tell me, Lucia, what did you mean? What distressed you so?"

"Distressed! Of course I was, to see you lying there, so still, so pale." There was a touch of defiance in her voice, but her eyes were avoiding his, he noticed.

"Tell me, Sister — about the tall, thin man who is causing all these accidents to Nicky and Serena?"

Shock made her face taut as she sat there, stunned to silence. And then her features crumpled and it all came pouring out.

"I gave him money for expenses, but — oh Roberto — I only wanted him to scare them away — make Serena go back home — take Nicky away from here."

Roberto's face was as black as thunder clouds as he urged her on, demanding to know all.

"Who is this man?" he snapped.

"The brother of that girl killed in Gino's car. I met him in London; he wanted to get his own back, but I never meant him to *harm* them, truly. But it seems he wanted revenge. He wouldn't go away when I begged him." As her face distorted, slow tears streaked down her ravaged cheeks. "I'm frightened; he's threatening me now." She sobbed noisily. "Please forgive me, Roberto."

"Never," he rasped. "Well not for a long time. I want you to pack your things at once, Lucia and take the next plane to Portugal. I'll arrange for cousins in Lisbon to give you a place with our connections there. Probably they'll find you a suitable husband!" His voice brooked no refusal.

"No. Oh no . . . "

"It's either that or a convent, Lucia. I'm ringing the police shortly to put them on to your man accomplice."

"You can't," she gasped, agitated. "He'll tell them about me!" Roberto shrugged against the pillows.

"It will be his word against mine. And you'll be far away by then."

She hung her head, defeated. He was the real head of the family and meant every word he said.

"You won't tell the old ones?" she begged.

"Of course not, but Serena must know all about this — her mind must be eased."

"She'll never forgive me," Lucia sobbed.

"I don't want you back here until the year's mourning for Gino has passed. *Capisco?*"

"Oh, Roberto . . . " she begged.

But he went on sternly, "I understand you very well. You thought the inheritance split in half is much more than divided into three, didn't you?"

Again she stretched out a pleading hand, but he ignored it.

"Go, Lucia. Get out of my sight."

With a sob she turned and left the room, leaving her brother with a dark shadow on his face.

Later that day, he told Serena everything.

"Lucia? How could she!" Her shock and disgust matched his, but he begged her to understand.

"Lucia adored Gino. I think the grief of his sudden death must have unhinged her mind. But don't worry, *cara*, I've sent her away for at least a year. It's either that or a convent, I told her." And the deep anger in his voice was all too easy to see. "Don't be sorry for her, dearest — she also loves money too well!"

Once more he spread his arms wide, and she was glad to feel them and their warmth around her; to feel his kisses, his tenderness.

"Soon we must talk, my dear one, but for now . . ."

She gave Nicky a lesson after lunch, and when Roberto came down, the little boy was fascinated by the huge multi-coloured lump on his uncle's forehead.

"Does it hurt, Zio?" he asked avidly.

"A little, that's all. But tell me, *piccolo*, will you still want to ride your pony?"

For a moment, undecided, Nicky bit his lip, and then nodded his head.

"Of course, it wasn't his fault, was it?"

"You're a brave boy, Nico." The praise made the little chest swell with pleasure.

All was peacefully quiet after dinner, except for the sound of the crickets in the garden. Nicky had put away his latest jigsaw puzzle and gone to bed. Oriana Ercoli sat with a piece of crochet work, and her husband dozed gently over his newspaper.

Glancing across at Roberto, Serena

saw him give a signal, pointing first to her and then at himself and finally up to the ceiling. She nodded, smiling at the wicked glint in his eyes. With an exaggerated yawn, she rose, kissed her in-laws goodnight and left the room.

Twenty minutes later, Roberto did the same. As he closed the bedroom door behind him, he turned to see Serena's sparkling eyes peeping at him from beneath the cover.

Hurriedly discarding his clothes, he slid into the bed beside her, peering under the sheet at her naked body, feigning surprise! She giggled and snuggled closer.

"I know — but I couldn't wait," she whispered. As if aroused by her eagerness, he began to make love to her more fiercely, more wildly than before. Answering passion made her respond, and after they reached an explosive climax together, they both lay exhausted and exultant. For both of them, there had never been such lovemaking.

And Roberto looked down at her — his cool, fair-haired, ice princess with her smooth brow and fine cheekbones; yet inside, she was like a smouldering volcano waiting for the right touch to make her erupt into blazing passion.

She stirred indolently after a while and told him, "We can't keep doing this, Roberto. What if someone found out, found me in your bed?"

How could she tell him of thoughts passing through her mind — the knowledge that he'd said he wanted her, but had never mentioned the future? Had she made yet another mistake? Did he want them to marry?

As if reading those turbulent thoughts, he answered softly, "We can't get married, *cara*. I can't make you *mia moglie* — not for another year. For the sake of my parents and Gino, we must wait the year of mourning for him."

He tenderly kissed the slender shoulder next to his.

"But I must have you with me, here in my bed." His words were quietly possessive, thrilling her with their intensity. "It won't be easy, *adorata*, but with patience and love, we can eventually sort out and solve the problems."

And quietly he suggested just what they might do. That they spend half the year in Italy and the rest in London.

"Soon Nico will be old enough to go to boarding-school." At that Serena stirred beside him, so he hastened on, "Or as a weekly boarder. Lettie can still care for him, keep on the apartment for us to use over there. He can spend all the holidays here — the flight is only about two hours long and there are airports at each end."

In his haste to convince her, his words came out jumbled, but she got his meaning.

"That way, we get the best of both worlds, for all of us. My parents are getting older. Nico will grow up to know about wines and our vineyards, take his place in the firm. You will help too with your knowledge. I will need to travel in the UK and Europe — take Gino's place at the London office."

In her mind's eye, she could see it could be made to work — with care and understanding, give and take.

He didn't tell her that he wanted Lettie to stay on with them against the time when they would have their own children — sturdy sons like Nico and maybe a silver-haired little daughter like Serena. He knew it wouldn't be easy, but so many people commuted in these days of quick travel and double homes.

"I thought perhaps we could tell my parents, Lettie and Walter and no one else." She wriggled closer. "I still don't fancy slipping along the landings for the next twelve months. And I must be near to Nicky a little longer." She felt him give a wicked little chuckle.

"I've thought of that, too, *cara*. I'll have a door made there — in the wall between these rooms and Nico's. That way, you'll hear him; you'll do your 'slipping' through his little room to yours on the other side. See?"

"You want to be sure of your loving," she smiled, pressing soft lips along his jawline.

"Always, *cara*, for the rest of my life!" Such a declaration could only lead to more lovemaking; this time gently, with the exploration of every inch of her soft body.

"I'm going to write to Lettie in the morning. She'll be so happy for me, I know."

★ ★ ★

But in the post the next morning, she found a long letter from Lettie.

"Good news, *cara*?" Roberto had been watching her face, the delighted look in her eyes.

"The very best, darling. Lettie's going to marry Walter, my boss. I'm so pleased for both of them; they'll make such a fine couple. They've been so lonely . . . Walter will be keeping on his own little flat, but he'll share

300

Lettie's room sometimes too. Like us they'll have two homes."

She gathered the letter together, her face shining with happiness for these two dear people.

"I must ring Lettie tonight, when she's finished work and give my congratulations — tell her all about us."

She'll be surprised, Serena mused, thinking how angrily she had spoken about Roberto after his visit to the apartment. And yet, she recalled, even then she had felt the pull of attraction for him, hadn't she?

The plans for the party went ahead with momentum. Caterers were booked; phone calls and messages were sent to neighbours and friends and staff. Everyone was invited.

Of course it was to be held outdoors and already lights were being strung from tree to tree. Trestle tables and benches stacked ready; musicians of all sorts were persuaded to bring their instruments. Barrels of wine had been selected, one for each table.

Serena made a hurried trip down to Verona to choose a new dress. The cotton frocks she had brought with her suddenly didn't seem good enough. She spent a hot, sticky morning in and out of the best boutiques trying on garments, finding it hard to decide which she liked best. Somehow the black one seemed dowdy, so she finally picked one in pale lavender touched with silver. It had shoe-string shoulder straps in silver, showing off her smooth tanned shoulders; with a softly flounced skirt. In fine crepe, it suited her colouring to perfection. In a little back street, she found a pair of sandals, thin and strippy with high heels.

And, as a final purchase, she bought a new white evening shirt for Nicky — one with lace down the front, and just hoped she could persuade him into wearing it!

★ ★ ★

She had just touched her eyelids with pale lavender-coloured shadow when Roberto gave her bedroom door a quick rap and then walked in.

Through the mirror she saw his face as he looked across the room at her.

"Bellissima, cara," he murmured, dropping a fervent kiss on one bare shoulder. "I'll be so proud of you, Serena."

"You look rather dishy yourself, darling," she replied. In fact, the sight of him there, tall, dark and splendid in his well-cut evening suit, the pristine white shirt emphasizing his dark tan, had made her heart lift with loving pride. Side by side, reflected in the heavy old mirror, they did make a really handsome couple.

"Come, *cara*, we have time to tell the parents about us."

Serena, her heart beating rapidly, watched her in-laws' faces nervously as Roberto quietly, proudly, told them that in a year's time he and Serena would marry. Told them of the plans to spend time there and in London.

She watched, too, the look of puzzlement on her son's young face.

"So you will be my papa — not my uncle?"

"That is so, Nico. Will that please you?"

For a second there was silence, time for contemplation, and then he burst out, "Yes, yes!" and he ran to hug Roberto round the legs, holding him close.

Watching him playing with the local children, getting as dirty, as noisy as them, she knew he'd be happy in the life they had planned.

Piles of food disappeared; the wine flowed copiously; gossip, music, singing — under the darkening sky, the party still went on. Couples danced on rough lawns, arms entwined in a fast polka, pausing only to kiss or take more wine.

"I must tell you — the police have got your mystery man, so no more worrying, little one, about Nico, *si*?"

Serena came down from the clouds with a jerk.

"Nicky? I haven't seen him for ages."

"He's with the other *ragazzi*." But her eyes were already looking round anxiously.

They still hadn't found him two hours later and Serena was almost hysterical with worry. Had that wicked man finally succeeded in hurting him before the police had caught up with him? Her face was pale with anxiety, her cheeks blotched with tears.

Until at last, one of the labourers appeared carrying a sleeping Nicky in his arms. He had been found locked in one of the little rooms off the packing hall. A mischievous youngster had turned the key for a joke, and then been taken home by his parents, leaving Nicky's distraught family searching everywhere for him.

"I wanted to see in there," the drowsy boy mumbled, too sleepy to understand what his disappearance had done to his worried mother.

"The key should not have been in the door!" Roberto's face was dark with anger, feeling pity for his beloved's ordeal. Tomorrow, someone's head would roll for that! Tomorrow would see talk between Nico and his new father-to-be!

But as for tonight . . . with Nicky fast asleep upstairs, the Ercoli parents raised their glasses in a toast to Serena and Roberto, giving them their blessing. Feeling safe at last in his arms, Serena's heart bubbled with happiness — bubbled like the sparkling Asti Spumante.

Later, wrapped in each other's arms, they found once more their own private heaven — two halves were one.

★ ★ ★

It was June — a year later — and the gardens of Casa d'Ercoli were in full splendour to celebrate their marriage.

Long tables with snowy-white damask cloths were bedecked with flowers and trailing green vines. Fine china, silver cutlery, cut glass, all sparkled in the brilliant sunshine. Beneath an arch bearing the Ercoli coat of arms, entwined with fragrant roses, Serena and Roberto stood, receiving the congratulations, the kisses and handshakes of all their friends gathered there. In a beautiful long gown of apricot organza, a wreath of matching rosebuds in her hair, she had never looked more beautiful. Beside her, still proud and tall, Roberto looked happier than he had ever looked, in his light grey suit and pale blue shirt.

All around, the very air seemed laden with happiness as the guests queued to kiss the bridal couple. Mr and Mrs Tunnicliffe — Lettie and Walter — had come over with Serena's parents. Danielle's invitation had not yet caught up with her. Matthew Jamison's arm was adorned by an equally staid-looking Scots girl who hung on his every word! Maria Donati contentedly flashed an expensive engagement ring given her by the young Italian at her side. Nothing was heard from Lucia Ercoli, to everyone's relief!

And young Nicky was fast getting tired of being told how much he'd grown in a year; hated, too, the silk shirt his mother had insisted he wore instead of his favourite T-shirt! All the same, he joined the queue, and when he reached the happy couple, he stood looking up at Roberto, whose mouth suddenly became dry.

"*Congratulazione*, Roberto." He put out his small hand solemnly. "Now I shall call you Papa!"

With equal solemnity, Roberto shook the hand, swallowing the lump in his throat before answering, "And from now on, Nico, I shall call you my son." And for a long moment, dark eyes looked into dark eyes, and then they hugged each other close before Nicky turned to his mother.

★ ★ ★

The moon was bright and full; the pale-winged moths were flirting with the coloured lights in the trees. Older guests were gradually dispersing, and the bridal pair had already slipped away to their bedroom — the Rose Room.

As Roberto came from the bathroom, he saw Serena standing dreaming at the long window. The moonlight made her hair a silver halo. He could see every lovely curve of her body showing through the diaphanous new nightie, and felt the familiar urge in his loins . . .

She turned, her face soft with love, languorous with anticipation — and a little too much wine! And as she glanced at the big old bed, she gave a wicked little chuckle.

"The same bed," she murmured. "Nothing's different tonight . . . "

He crossed over and stood before her; with gentle hands he pushed the straps from her shoulders, and the glamorous nightie slithered to the floor.

"You are wrong, *carrissima mia*,

tonight is different. For tonight we make our first *bambino*."

And they did . . . !

THE END

WITH SOMEBODY ELSE
Theresa Charles

Rosamond sets off for Cornwall with Hugo to meet his family, blissfully unaware of the shocks in store for her.

A SUMMER FOR STRANGERS
Claire Hamilton

Because she had lost her job, her flat and she had no money, Tabitha agreed to pose as Adam's future wife although she believed the scheme to be deceitful and cruel.

VILLA OF SINGING WATER
Angela Petron

The disquieting incidents that occurred at the Vatican and the Colosseum did not trouble Jan at first, but then they became increasingly unpleasant and alarming.

DOCTOR NAPIER'S NURSE
Pauline Ash

When cousins Midge and Derry are entered as probationer nurses on the same day but at different hospitals they agree to exchange identities.

A GIRL LIKE JULIE
Louise Ellis

Caroline absolutely adored Hugh Barrington, but then Julie Crane came into their lives. Julie was the kind of girl who attracts men without even trying.

COUNTRY DOCTOR
Paula Lindsay

When Evan Richmond bought a practice in a remote country village he did not realise that a casual encounter would lead to the loss of his heart.

ENCORE
Helga Moray

Craig and Janet realise that their true happiness lies with each other, but it is only under traumatic circumstances that they can be reunited.

NICOLETTE
Ivy Preston

When Grant Alston came back into her life, Nicolette was faced with a dilemma. Should she follow the path of duty or the path of love?

THE GOLDEN PUMA
Margaret Way

Catherine's time was spent looking after her father's Queensland farm. But what life was there without David, who wasn't interested in her?